THE DAREDEVIL SURGEON RISKS IT ALL

KRISTINE LYNN

MEDICAL ROMANCE

Recycling programs for this product may not exist in your area.

ISBN-13: 978-1-335-95286-8

The Daredevil Surgeon Risks It All

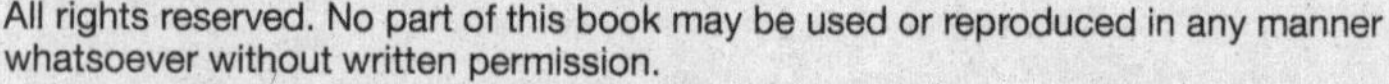

For questions and comments about the quality of this book, please contact us at CustomerService@Harlequin.com.

Harlequin Enterprises ULC
22 Adelaide St. West, 41st Floor
Toronto, Ontario M5H 4E3, Canada
www.Harlequin.com

HarperCollins Publishers
Macken House, 39/40 Mayor Street Upper,
Dublin 1, D01 C9W8, Ireland
www.HarperCollins.com

Printed in U.S.A.

1 2 3 4 5 6 7 8 9 10 HDC 29 28 27 26

A brand-new trilogy from Kristine Lynn!

High Altitude Docs

You've reached the peak of medicine...

Welcome to Washington's Olympic Mountains, where the extreme terrain attracts the most fearless climbers—and the most daredevil docs!

Mountain medic Erin plans to take emergency medicine in the region to even greater heights... *if* she can convince city doc Reese to sign off on it. Will a week stranded in the wilderness win him over?

Surgeon brothers Ian and Greg have escaped their city lifestyles looking for adventure and find it working at Erin and Reese's new state-of-the-art medical facility. But for daredevil Dr. Ian, will getting close to nurse Casey be the biggest risk of all?

Find out where it all began in Reese and Erin's story
City Doc to the Rescue

And in Ian and Casey's story
The Daredevil Surgeon Risks It All

Both available now!

And their legacy continues with Greg's story

Coming soon!

Dear Reader,

Welcome back to the Olympic Range for book two of High Altitude Docs! I'm excited to explore more of the backcountry with you—and the true adventure of falling in love!

Dr. Ian Matthews thrives on conquering the riskiest medical cases, ski slopes and rugged peaks. Originally from Chicago, he tackled genetic abnormality issues no one would touch. After a major loss on a case, he's happy to trade that world of medicine for the Hector Ruiz Medical Center in the mountains.

When a local boy is brought in by his mom with a case similar to what killed Ian's sister and a patient in Chicago, he's terrified. It's why he left genetic medicine, and why he won't let anyone get close to him. Close equals loss.

Too bad the boy's risk-averse mom, Casey, is the clinic's new nurse. As she works alongside Ian, she weakens his resolve to keep love at arm's length and pursue the medicine he was so good at in this forced-proximity, opposites-attract story.

I look forward to your thoughts on Ian and Casey, and their adventure in love. Drop me a line on Instagram or Facebook, or by email at kristinelynnauthor@gmail.com.

Thanks for reading!

XO, *Kristine*

Hopelessly addicted to espresso and HEAs, **Kristine Lynn** pens high-stakes romances in the wee morning hours before teaching writing at an Oregon college. Luckily, the stakes there aren't as dire. When she's not grading, writing, or searching for the perfect vanilla latte, she can be found on the hiking trails behind her home with her daughter and puppy. She'd love to connect on X, Facebook or Instagram.

Books by Kristine Lynn

Harlequin Medical Romance

Royal York Hospital

Wedding Date with Dr. Petrides

Paging Dr. Morrison

Doctor's Nine-Month Rival

High Altitude Docs

City Doc to the Rescue

Brought Together by His Baby
Accidentally Dating His Boss
Their Six-Month Marriage Ruse
A Kiss with the Irish Surgeon
Nine Months to Marry the Princess
How to Resist Your Enemy

Visit the Author Profile page at Harlequin.com.

For Amy and Julia. Your photos and stories of the Olympic backcountry helped shape these pages of adventure, while your love for one another helped me imagine the greater adventure of love my characters undertake. Keep exploring forever.

CHAPTER ONE

IAN MATTHEWS STARED out over the canyon and let the trace amounts of fear dissipate like nitrogen in his blood after a deep scuba dive. The tension in his shoulders acted as a trigger that he should pay attention.

And he was—make no mistake. Hell, at the edge of Hurricane Ridge, the wind whipping around him, spraying his face with icy water, a vast canyon filled with fog that obscured the treacherous trail leading back to Hoodsport, he paid attention or he died.

As a surgeon, he knew that fear was nothing more than his amygdala firing off messages to his brain that he was in danger. That knowledge didn't keep the whisper of nerves that danced up his spine and opened his airways at bay. He knew the trail, knew its perils, but he was still scared. And smart to be.

The fear had kept him alive, so far.

But danger was what he was after, out here in the Olympic backcountry at least. It was his release from the day-to-day where he had to play it safe, when others' lives were at risk. He wouldn't ever play roulette with them again—not to satisfy his need to push the limits or prove he knew his stuff.

Nothing was worth the crippling guilt that came with holding the bill of sale for a price someone else had paid with their life.

No, he'd take out his adventure-seeking on the trails, slopes and seas of the Pacific Northwest. It was safer. Sort of.

A crack of thunder echoed off the canyon walls, deep and angry. That meant rain up the canyon to the west, which meant the possibilities of flash flooding in the canyon floors below him.

As long as he listened to his body and honored its limits, listened to the clash of weather and earth and estimated his course of action based on the alchemy, he'd be fine.

Basically, as long as he wasn't an idiot, he wouldn't end up dead, or worse.

He tightened the pack's straps around his waist since he'd be heading downhill and his weight would shift to his hips. At least this was the last day of his four-day trek and the food and water were depleted to his reserves. Things were always lighter on the way down.

"Okay," he said out loud. "Let's get this done so we can see what Greg's been bugging me about." He'd gotten half a dozen notifications when he was in and out of the spotty service, but he never had enough of a digital connection to see what they contained.

Ian and his brother had a secret code with their third medical partner, Reese Vallen, a pediatrician from Seattle who'd come to Hoodsport to live with his fiancée, Erin. If one of the three of them sent two texts in their group chat back-to-back, it meant there was trouble. Whoever was out of range getting the notifications was supposed to use the sat phone to check in. But there was nothing on the group chat, so it could wait.

Ian scrambled down a rocky outcrop, careful not to land on the wet mossy patches of the boulders. The Pacific Northwest—especially the area around Hoodsport and the Olympic Range—was a temperate rainforest, meaning it was perpetually damp, if not sopping.

At first, Ian had worried the weather would wear him down. If not the rain, then the darkness that settled in over the coastal range for four months out of the year. The rest of the time, the sky was a dull gray, with high, overhead clouds that draped over Mount Rainier and Puget Sound, a cozy blanket that was also stiflingly without light.

But that hadn't been the case. First of all, those dark days were gloomy, sure, but when the sun came out and the whole valley shone like an emerald jewel, it more than made up for the gray. Mount Rainier would peek out from behind its blanket of clouds and the Salish Sea would sparkle a pale teal; it was as if he lived in the Caribbean. It was so damn perfect it made Ian's breath catch every time it happened.

The rest of the time, on days like today, for example, where he played slalom between the waves of bone-chilling fog as he traversed the canyon, he sucked it up and found the beauty in the swirling weather.

Ian had learned in the past year how to get out and enjoy the myriad treasures the area offered him no matter the forecast. The trick was to dress for the weather and then the world was his playground.

And what a playground it was. Adventure awaited him around every bend in the rivers, each hill or peak he summited. He loved his new home, the job included.

It was rare for him to get excited to go back to work, or at least that was the case before he'd packed up and moved to Washington state and joined the Hector Ruiz Clinic as one of three primary trauma surgeons.

Before that move, he'd taken a leave of absence from surgery, which had been necessary to get his head right, to come back to medicine at all. It seemed like a lifetime ago, even though the reverberations of the leave—and what had precipitated it—were still there, brewing beneath his skin. He wasn't complaining. They kept him on his toes and made sure he paid attention.

And it's not like he was "back" in the same way

as he'd been before, in Chicago. He didn't think he'd ever take on that level of complex surgeries ever again, and he wasn't complaining about that, either.

Being an orthopedic physician out here was different from Chicago. Not easier. Not with the mountains and recreational waterways that gave people the opportunity to explore the beauty of the outdoors—and the occasional broken bone as a reminder of how unforgiving Mother Nature could be. Chicago had been more intense. Cases that had challenged him and helped turn him into the surgeon he was today, sure. But it had been all work, all the time. And the kind of cases that kept him up at night, thinking about what he might've done differently. Well, one, anyway.

Here, he had balance.

He saw enough fractures and gnarly breaks to satisfy his medical curiosity. But they also were infrequent enough that he was able to take on orthopedic cases for Mason County. Nothing risky—those days were in his past. Just enough to make sure he gave back to the community that had taken them all in and welcomed them as if they were born and raised in the area.

He hopped over a downed fir that must have been a hundred years old. Chances were a windstorm felled the beast after the dry summer they'd had last year. Even the Olympic Peninsula—historically one of the wettest places on the planet—was susceptible to the changing climates happening all across the globe.

They'd better keep an eye on that with hikers in the park this summer. He ran down the trail when it smoothed out, his thumbs hooked in his pack. Just as he got to the bottom, he slowed down, and thank goodness he did. A black-tailed deer and its fawn darted onto the trail just feet in front of him and startled when they caught sight of him. He tried to stop, to give them room to move around him, but wasn't prepared for the abrupt shift in speed and direction. He felt the slip happening but was powerless to stop it. The traction on his boots didn't catch the grit on the rocks and his feet slid out from under him. He was on his side before he could assess what had happened, other than the searing pain he felt on his right side. The two deer just hopped away, none the wiser to his fall or injury.

Ian struggled to catch his breath; it'd been knocked out of him so thoroughly.

On one hand, he was grateful for the truck-sized boulder that stopped him from going over the edge of the embankment. That would have been a bummer of a way to lose a leg—or end up unconscious.

But the wall of rock also acted like a sledgehammer against his side, hitting him against the frame of his backpack. He tried to get up, but pain shot up his right leg from his shin. A glance down showed he'd torn through his hiking pants and sliced open his leg. It wasn't catastrophic, but it'd need immediate attention when he got back.

"Dammit," he said. He righted himself and sat on the patch of rock where he'd landed as he fashioned a makeshift bandage out of his bandana. First, he cleaned the wound with alcohol he kept in the side of his pack. "Not cool," he hissed. It burned something fierce. He growled as he fitted the bandage, but it would be fine till he got off the mountain. He'd just have to take it slow so he didn't pull another bonehead move.

He sent a text to his brother and Reese even though it wouldn't go through until he was closer to town. Glancing at his watch, he estimated that would be a solid six hours from now—on two good legs. He stretched and winced.

He'd need more like eight. Better to get started so he didn't end up finishing in the dark, too. The walk down was arduous but nothing he hadn't done at one point or another. Still, he had no plans to end up like his patients—lost and injured in the wilderness—but this had been a close call. It went to show that even Ian, with a backpack of contingencies and lifetime of experience, could fall victim to the elements.

Seven hours later he hit the trailhead and was met at the edge of the parking lot with what had to be a mirage. It wasn't quite dusk, and the fog had thinned down in the valley, so it couldn't be a trick of his eyes. Still, it didn't make sense.

A tall blonde, hair up in a tight ponytail, leaned against his rig, a fitted OR jacket over jeans hugging curves that made his mouth dry. She stared at him as if she knew who he was, or like she'd been expecting him. He'd be damned if her jade-green eyes didn't pierce something raw in his chest.

He approached the truck, but she didn't move or offer an explanation. Just took in his ripped pants and hastily bandaged leg. He felt sticky under the fabric, meaning the wound still wasn't closing. Damn. He might need stitches.

That was later-Ian's problem. This version needed a shower, a whiskey and a look at the wound under better light—and not in that order.

"Excuse me," he said, dropping his bag at her feet. Just in case his mind wasn't totally clear from the last few hours on a bum leg and several days of walking in the wilderness alone before that, he checked the license plate. Nope. It was his truck, alright. "I need to get in here."

Her arms were crossed over her chest, and he tried to focus on her mouth instead of a peek at the cleavage showing in the deep V of the open-zippered jacket. She was beautiful; he'd give her that. Even if her scowl said she was frustrated. With him? It didn't make sense since he didn't know who the hell she was.

The mystery woman jutted out a hip but still didn't move.

"You *need* to take care of that leg. The clinic

is an hour from here and it's impossible to drive a stick shift with a laceration like the one you described."

Her voice was familiar and ran under his skin like a current. But try as he might, he couldn't place where he might've heard it before. Damn, he wished he wasn't exhausted, dehydrated and nursing an injury that likely needed treatment. Which she seemed in agreement about.

Too bad he didn't have a clue who she was or why she'd care about his leg. Hell, or how she knew about his clinic. This was turning out to be the strangest day of his life.

He stared at her, mouth agape. "Sorry," he said, running a hand through his hair. "I don't know who you are."

There was a flash of surprise on her face, where her lips became full almost-smiling things. But before he could get used to how damn captivating the woman was when she didn't look poised to slap him, it was back to annoyance in her pulled brows and frown.

Unfortunately, she was still captivating, albeit a little intense.

"Casey Larsen. Your new nurse practitioner." He blanched. *She* was their new nurse? She was…well, stunning. Attractive. *And off-limits*, his intrusive inner critic chimed in.

"Oh, got it. I'm Ian Matthews, which I'm guessing you know."

"Yep. You're the first person I spoke to about the open position, right? You and Dr. Vallen?" She got in her rig and while she fished around for something, he tried not to look at the way she filled out those jeans, but it was futile. She was like a magnet, pulling his focus. How interesting she was just as alluring in the flesh as she'd been on the phone.

He thought about that first interview with Casey. She'd interviewed with Greg and Erin in person in Seattle, but Reese and Ian had planned a ski trip to tackle a dozen of the hundred and sixty trails in Olympic Park so they'd taken the preliminary phone calls instead. If he was being honest, during the application process, he'd liked the easy way she spoke about her work with no fluff or arrogance. Just awareness that she was damned good at what she did. Seeing her in person—that same easy confidence wafting off her—was distracting.

"That's right. I'm glad you got the offer." He winced. That was way too personal, especially since his body had certainly chimed in about its appreciation of her—and none of it had to do with the skills she'd expressed on her phone interview.

"I'm glad to be here. You guys have done a good job getting the clinic up and running—we've been busy this whole week."

Guilt at having left during a busy week was coupled with another, more personal, guilt. He'd missed her whole onboarding? How had that happened?

"You got in early." It was a statement more than a question. He'd thought he was a hundred percent sure she was arriving two days after his backpacking trip was supposed to end.

A shadow passed over her face, and if he didn't know any better, he'd say whatever had brought it also carried pain in its wake. He recognized that kind of hurt expression—the kind he'd carried the first year after his…after the event that had forced him to take a leave of absence.

"I had a personal thing come up and needed to push up my arrival. Greg agreed I could start early once my…issue was resolved."

His curiosity piqued. He wanted to ask, to get to know the new nurse—Casey—who had him captive with her voice, her presence… But then he glanced around.

Reality set in. He was at the trailhead after a week off-grid, was unshowered, hungry and bleeding from a significant wound on his leg—not at the office prepared to have this conversation.

Ian shook his head, trying to chase the fog away, but between the ache in his leg and his overall sore body, he wasn't tracking what was going on. Not at all.

"Sorry, Casey, but why are you here? Did Greg want us to meet?" And if he did, why'd his brother choose that location? Why right after his hike? He didn't mind the unexpected—to him, anyway—meeting, but he couldn't figure out why they were there. Nothing was making sense. "I'm glad to meet you, but a little exhausted—I've been out almost all week."

"You didn't get the texts from him?"

He shook his head, but as he did, his phone chimed three, four, then a series of times back-to-back. At least that cleared something up. He'd just gotten back into service.

"Those are probably the context we both need." He ignored his phone, though, more interested in the woman physically in front of him than what his brother had to say about her. Something about those eyes demanded his focus and attention, even if the circumstances didn't make sense… He'd catch up on his missed messages at home once he got back.

"I know. Just like I know you fell this morning and need medical attention. This isn't a meet and greet, Doc." He glanced over at her. How did she know about his fall? She pointed to her phone, and he grimaced. Another mystery that would have been answered if he'd gotten the unchecked messages before he made it to the trailhead. But how had she found out about the injury if none of his texts had arrived till just then? "Your brother got your messages about your cut and asked me to come out here to be your nurse."

His brows raised and he hated that his tired body betrayed him by grinning like an idiot when she mentioned being his new nurse. His imagination didn't need much prompting to envision what her caring for him could look like. She seemed to have picked up on that, and as the sun slipped behind the first peak on the horizon, he couldn't be sure if it was the neon pink of the sky or her embarrassment that caused her cheeks to appear red.

"I mean, since I'm the new nurse practitioner at the Hector Ruiz Clinic and your brother's gone, he asked me to meet you here and help you with your—" She gestured to his leg, and he had to admit he kinda liked that she was as flummoxed as he was all of a sudden. It put them on more even ground.

"My injury." She nodded, her eyes bright.

"Yes," she said, finding something interesting in the dirt at her feet. "That."

"Got it," he said. Her cheeks reddened even more. He didn't say more, just stared back at her. He didn't know why, but having her there, in his world, threw it off its axis, even if it was just the parking lot. Maybe he needed to add sleep to that list. Either way, spending more time in close proximity to a woman he was drawn to didn't seem like the best idea—especially in his exhausted state. "Um, but anyway, I think I'm good to go. In terms of needing help. I'll just—"

He'd what? Fix it himself?

Her brows raised as if to ask the same question.

"What are you thinking?" he asked. "This isn't exactly a sterile field."

"I was thinking I'd get a ride back to your place

and I can clean and disinfect and get a better sense of things. I know we just met, but your company vetted me and—"

"My place is on the other side of the Hood Canal." Meaning it would add forty minutes to their drive, past the clinic.

She seemed to weigh this, giving him another visual once-over as if that was enough to decide that he wasn't going to murder her in her own home.

"Fine," she finally said. She walked to the driver's side of her truck and climbed in. "We'll go to mine. But I'm driving and I'll take you to pick up your truck tomorrow." She hesitated. What was she thinking through? "You can stay in my guest room. I don't trust that leg of yours for an hour's drive on winding backroads."

He didn't, either. And he'd never had an easy time trusting others, especially when relying on his own efforts meant less room for error. As it always did when he considered collaborating with another doctor, nurse or even fellow climber, his past loomed tall in his rearview mirror.

Maybe if his sister's care had been in the hands of someone capable, she'd still be with them. A stab of regret made him flinch—she'd have loved the hike he just completed. But she'd never even gotten to go to her first high school dance, let alone explore the world. The injustice of it all—of her loss and the compounding effect on him and Greg—was crippling if he just sat around and thought about it. So, he didn't. He got out, he sought adventure on her behalf, and even with an injury like he had now, it was always worth it—the living while he was able.

Yeah, but if you'd had help that day in the OR, maybe you wouldn't have missed the heart issue.

He shivered despite the warmth of the late afternoon. The "heart issue" his intrusive dickhead of a subconscious called up was a fluke aortic aneurysm that had ultimately killed his young patient without warning. It shouldn't have been there, shouldn't have happened, especially given his age. It'd been a routine osteogenesis imperfecta bone setting, and the kid hadn't left the table. His family had gone home without their son.

Dammit. Why'd he have to think of that now? He'd made so much progress…

Ian's skin itched and despite his exhaustion, he had the impulse to head right back down the trail he'd just left, but that wasn't possible. He went through a round of box breathing instead.

The only thing that Ian had ever come up with was that he should have somehow caught it. Or if someone else was on the boy's care, maybe they would have. No one—not Greg, not even the hospital board—agreed with that, but it still drove him to near madness until he'd taken his leave of absence to get his head back in the game.

His ability to trust others in his efforts hadn't improved much, except at least he was open to it enough to join this practice and to invite docs and nurses into his space that he'd never met. Somehow, though, handing over his care to this woman he'd never met, had barely spoken to, was effortless. Hmm. Maybe that bode well for working with her in the clinic.

Yeah, if you can stop ogling her.

He wasn't ogling her—he was just thirsty. Hungry. Tired as hell. Once he rested, he'd forget he ever thought of her as anything other than a colleague.

"Okay," he finally said, "but we're stopping for burgers on me on the way home. I'm starving."

"That's fine. Any preference of places or can I go to O'Connor's?"

O'Connor's Pub had the best burgers in town. "Nope. That's perfect."

He got in the passenger side of her truck, moving his gear to the bed as she winced.

"I didn't mean to make that face," she said by way of explanation. "It's just a new truck and I'm trying to take care of it."

He felt bad. It was a nice truck, smaller than his and with a shine his hadn't had since the minute he'd left the lot with it. To him, trucks—and backpacks, tents, climbing gear, all of it—were tools for the real thing of value. *Living.*

What did she value? He had an intrusive thought that he'd like to find out, even if it was the worst idea imaginable. He finally had life just as he wanted it. Adding a woman to the mix, a woman who was so different from him at first glance, wasn't the way to keep the delicate balance of work and adventure he'd cultivated to keep the demons at bay.

That burger and some sleep couldn't come soon enough.

"I'm sorry." He pulled out a rain cover from his pack, sliding it beneath his filthy leg. "I'll clean up if there's a mess, later."

Any kind of mess he left behind with his presence.

Adventure was his therapy, his way of working through his thoughts and pushing aside the ones that threatened to derail his progress. Dating a woman—any woman—was too close to that idea of collaboration for what he needed, so he'd never let himself go there before. Hookups with women who were of the same mindset as him? Definitely. Sating certain needs was necessary from time to time. But letting someone into his heart *and* his bed?

No thanks. There was too much emotional wreckage for someone to trip over.

He'd thought the trail he'd taken—a new one for him—was the pinnacle of adventure he'd find in the Pacific Northwest. But now, sitting next to a clean, beautiful—albeit too polished for his taste—woman who, in close quarters smelled like the wild daisies and lupine he'd walked through on day two of his trek, he reconsidered.

Had he missed something by going after every sunset, every trip, every surgery alone? He didn't think so. It was a system that had worked for him so far.

While he thought about that, he rolled down the window, citing car sickness, which he'd never actually had in his life.

He just couldn't inhale more of that scent without thinking that maybe…

Maybe he didn't know a thing about actual adventure.

He distracted himself by swiping open his phone and sure enough, he had a few missed texts. One from his buddy Ethan in Manhattan sharing the scans of his mom's bone cancer. It looked like the tumors were shrinking, but Ian would need to see them blown up and with the right backlighting. There were half a dozen messages from Reese—nothing big, though. Just updates on Ian's patient who'd broken her foot while trying to learn slacklining… At sixty. He had to love the sense of adventure but advised her that it would be best to take up hobbies that kept at least one foot on the ground at all times.

He checked the texts from Greg. Sure enough, there was a string of explanations, not only of who the woman propping up his truck was, but other changes to his brother's life in the past week.

The new nurse practitioner's credentials were cleared. She arrives Monday, starts soon after that. Her name is Casey Larsen and she's got a son in kindergarten. You'll like her sass, if it's not directed at you.

Oh, and the mutt outside the clinic's name is Scout. I'm adopting him. Congrats on becoming an uncle. Again.

Ian shook his head. *Great.* Now he'd be roped into dog-sitting when his brother took off to the less adventurous vacations he craved. Greg wasn't as into the thrill-chasing as Ian, preferring calm to chaos and planning versus spontaneity.

And yet, the guy still hadn't seemed to grasp that a through trail loop wasn't finished on a certain day, but when he got done. Like, today. Now.

The next text gave more information about why Casey had been standing at his truck.

Just got your text about your injury. That sucks, bud. I'm guessing you don't need help getting off the mountain or you would've said something, but if you're back tonight, the clinic'll be closed. Reese and Erin are in Seattle at that concert celebrating her first year as an internist. I'm heading to the city for a meeting with the board about the installation of the new CT scanner. If you're back after that, I'm gonna send Casey to see if you need stitches.

That's nonnegotiable. Good luck, brother. See ya Monday.

Great. His brother's seemingly good deed was in direct conflict with what Ian had been out there to do—chase adventure of the brand that he could control.

And now, her vanilla scent intoxicating him even with the window down, he was worried that maybe, if he wasn't careful, he'd find out he'd been going about it all wrong.

CHAPTER TWO

CASEY LARSEN OPENED the door to her new home, gesturing the grungy doctor inside. Even when he took his boots off at the front door, she could see the mud he left behind from his socks with each step. She held her breath to keep from saying anything. Because what could he do? Wait outside and let her stitch him under the front porch light in the fog?

This was my idea, she reminded herself. *I said yes to Greg when he asked.*

Why had she, again? So what if this was her first week at the job? Surely that didn't mean she had to say yes to each wacky assignment passed down to her…

It sort of did. She'd known good and well what she was getting into taking a job in rural, back-country Washington. It wasn't going to be a normal nine-to-five, which suited her, really.

Not only because of her son Henry's health issues that demanded a degree of flexibility in her work schedule, but because this job allowed her to shake off the mundaneness that crept in other areas of her life. For a long time—long before motherhood had claimed her—she'd traveled and explored at a pace all her own.

Nursing not only opened the door to her passion for medicine, but made sure the road beyond was varied and exciting.

But this? Inviting a man she'd never met into her home? Surely it constituted hazard pay.

He delicately laid down his pack on the tile floor, but it sagged against her beige matelassé couch. A light mud-colored dampness beaded on the top of the pack and trickled down to the couch.

He snatched it up and, giving her an apologetic glance, moved the pack to the front door. At least it would be easier to clean off the door paint rather than her furniture.

"Has the bleeding stopped?" she asked, her question only in part tinged with worry that he'd bleed on her pristine living room set. Why she'd brought her desert furniture to the wettest place in America was beyond her…

"Not quite." Ian grimaced, as if in apology. *Just don't sit down and I'll be fine. I mean, you'll be fine.*

"Hmm. Well, in my opinion, you should shower and rinse off the rest of the grime so it doesn't wash into a clean and sutured wound and infect the site. I'll use antiseptic either way after your shower."

Ian cleared his throat and ran a hand through his

hair. She ignored the sand that fell to her floor. He stared at his bag and shifted uncomfortably.

"I, uh, don't have a clean change of clothes. I wasn't really expecting anything other than heading home with my week's worth of grime." He shrugged and his crooked smile took her off guard, snuck past her senses. Which is probably why she responded the way she did.

"Let's just worry about the wound. I'll leave out some clean clothes you can use while I dress your injury, okay?" As soon as the words were out of her mouth, she regretted them. The clothes in question were a set of matching sleep pants that she'd bought Lawrence, her husband, for Christmas the month before he'd died.

Why hadn't she given them away with the rest of his belongings when she'd donated his things to the local shelter?

You know why. You felt guilty for giving everything away.

That wasn't entirely true, either. She felt guilty for *not* feeling guilty. Not about giving his half of their life away to whoever needed it now that he was gone. Not about wishing she'd left the loveless marriage years before, when it had become apparent he wasn't the husband or father she and Henry needed. Not about leaving his funeral dry-eyed.

She'd made an appointment the next day for a therapist, hoping to find out why she wasn't more heartbroken that the man she'd married had died.

Sure, they'd grown apart over the years, but it wasn't as if he'd just moved on… He was dead, and she didn't feel anything other than peace that she didn't have to worry about where he was or what he was doing as she had the last two years of their marriage while she'd raised their son. She wasn't much closer to an answer, either.

No, she knew just why she still had the holiday pajamas. Because she was in the same griefless rut she'd been in for two years.

A harder-to-answer question—why had she just offered the sleepwear to Ian?

He leaned against the door, seeming lost in thought. Finally, with a glance at his leg, he nodded. "Thanks. Where should I go?"

Casey led him to the guest bathroom in the back of the small craftsman. She'd bought the house sight unseen because of the tile and built-ins in the bathrooms. They looked to be original and in wonderful condition. If she hadn't been so passionate about medicine, she would have been a good real estate agent. Old homes held so much history and stories within their walls and she couldn't help waxing poetic about them.

She got him a towel, mentally noting that she should purchase some darker linens, too.

"All the soap is fair game and take your time. Make sure you get the wound nice and clean after you rinse."

"I know." She mentally recoiled. Of course he

did. He was a top-notch surgeon whose reputation preceded him. She, a nurse, didn't need to tell him about wound care. But then again, he was clearly a risk-taker, putting himself in situations where he might cause himself harm… Heck, he hadn't even been able to meet her for an interview because he was skiing or ice climbing or some other dangerous thing. And now he actually *had* hurt himself.

"Sorry. I know you're not a patient, that you know what you're doing." What she didn't say? That his propensity for play over work—and the ways that he reminded her of Lawrence—was her one holdup in talking to him about why she'd taken this job, in this place, with this surgeon.

"Thanks. And I'll make sure I clean up my mess when I'm done. I appreciate your help and don't want you to have more on your plate with this." He gestured to the whole of him and she shivered.

Of course he was talking about the half of Hurricane Ridge he'd brought in with him—pine needles included. No, she shivered because for some silly reason, her intrusive thoughts had her imagining the whole of him on her proverbial plate.

Sans clothes.

What was that about? She hadn't thought about a man with anything resembling lust—or worse, romance—in two years. Longer than that. Even the last few years of her marriage, she'd stopped seeing her husband that way. He loved Henry, of course, but she'd lost all respect for him when he didn't do anything to support their son's genetic abnormalities. That loss of respect had killed any passion between her and him.

So, why was she all of a sudden filled with warmth for a man she'd just met, a man who more closely resembled a walking Tasmanian devil than he did a human?

"It's fine. I'm not worried about the dirt. Let's just get your leg taken care of." She hoped her sincerity for the second part of her statement hid the lie from the first. It's not as if it was a total lie, either. As a nurse, she was surrounded by vomit and blood and far worse than a little dirt. But at home, she wanted it clean and tidy so Henry had less of a chance to slip and fall; at least that's what she told herself.

Her therapist had offered a different account. Lawrence had been messy in so many ways that Casey wanted her home to reflect the opposite now that he was gone.

That was probably true, too.

Gosh, she looked forward to putting her dead-end relationship behind her once and for all. When that might be—and what it might take—eluded her, though.

While he showered, she cleaned up the toys and blankets Henry had gotten out to build his fort. She smiled, missing her son, even knowing an overnight with his grandmother was a good thing for him. Casey's mom was still energetic, loved having fun exploring like a five-year-old boy wanted to but at the level that Henry's body could endure, and had the uncanny knack for picking just the right foods to match his moods. She would never be anything less than grateful that her mom had moved up here with them.

It was just so difficult to be away from Henry and worry about his health.

That was her trauma to heal from, though, not her son's.

She had to admit it was easier to keep her house clean when Henry wasn't sneaking newts and banana slugs into his room… She slumped on the edge of the couch and smiled.

White—even paint and tile—was beyond silly here in a land where everything was green and brown. To that end, perhaps she should rethink her whole layout. Her whole way of going about her losses.

I should have picked the crypton upholstery fabric—and a different husband. She couldn't help the latter—and wouldn't wish away anything that had given her the best thing in her life—but she could change her couches out. With Henry running around in the muddy rainforest and tracking in who-knew-what as he explored his new home, Casey had spent the past week cleaning the forest out of her home more than unpacking.

Making more work for herself wasn't exactly what the doctor—or her therapist, rather—ordered, but moving here did provide the opportunity for what Dr. Nylander had suggested. Namely, a fresh start where Henry could escape the pervasive and proverbial fog that followed him as the kid of a man killed when his twin-prop private plane crashed into the side of Mount Lemmon in Tucson.

Lawrence never should have been flying that day, but of course, who was she, the calm, conservative thinker, to tell him what good flight conditions looked like?

Anyway, he'd been gone two years now and it was time for all of them to move on. That was the one thing Casey and Dr. Nylander agreed on.

On the other hand, Casey moving her son to the center of wild country, where risk was inherent in crossing the street each day because one might encounter a bear, wolf or other wild animal? Let alone the type of medicine Casey was going to practice? Or where Henry would go to school? Well, what Dr. Nylander didn't know—yet—wouldn't hurt anyone.

Because some things were more important than taking on a little adventure. Henry's health was top of that list and Dr. Matthews—Ian, specifically—was the number one doctor for ortho abnormalities in the nation. That she'd had to track him down and move to the corner of the country, to a town she'd never heard of in an area she'd only seen on the cover of those outdoor magazines at the supermarket? That was unfortunate, but it wasn't as if she hadn't tried the traditional routes when he worked in Chicago.

She'd gotten a new-patient consultation for Henry and lived in excitement for the six months it took to get to the day before she and Henry were due to fly to Chicago and see what the doctor could do. Her son had been diagnosed with osteogenesis imperfecta, a genetic abnormality that made him more susceptible to breaks and fractures. It would impact the way he played, grew and even just moved through the world around him.

Only a handful of doctors could help reduce the effects and Dr. Matthews was one of them.

Casey's hands clenched in her lap as she recalled the phone call that had changed everything for her. For Henry. The day before their flight, she'd been adding Henry's medications to her and Lawrence's suitcase when her cell had rung with the osteo clinic's number flashing on her screen. She'd snatched it up and didn't think she'd ever forget the way a whole body tremor had shook from her core out when the assistant on the line canceled the appointment indefinitely.

"The doctor is taking an emergency leave of absence," she'd said. Even the assistant had sounded bereft. "We aren't sure when he'll return."

Casey remembered plugging in her phone, shutting the suitcase and sleeping until Lawrence got home from work. He'd listened as she'd cried but hadn't held her. Hadn't even brushed her shoulder with a calming touch.

"What will we do?" she'd asked.

"We wait it out. Who knows what'll change in the next few months or years with science. More docs will be able to help," he'd said with all the confidence she lacked. But then he'd started packing his own suitcase.

"Where are you going?" she'd wondered.

"I think I'll take Pete up on that Colorado River kayaking trip if you don't mind. Since I've already got the time off from work for this appointment, you know?"

She'd nodded numbly and watched her husband kiss their boy on the forehead and walk out like the air inside the small Arizona desert home was poisonous.

He'd died two weeks later. And Ian Matthews had all but vanished.

She shook her head free of the nightmare of her past and glanced at her watch. Ian had been in the shower almost half an hour now. They might live in the wettest part of the country, but her desert-living mindset hadn't transitioned yet.

She knocked on the door just as the water turned off. "Everything okay in there? Do you need anything?"

There was a rustle behind the door, then it opened, a cloud of steam escaping like the fog each morning over the valley. Casey gulped as Ian walked out, realizing it was more than a little dirt that had caked his skin.

Whatever disguise his hiking clothes and week's worth of not showering had created, it was off now and the man was in all his glory, close enough for her to reach out and touch.

And what glory it was. She tried swallowing, but darn if all the moisture in her body had fled… elsewhere. *South.*

"What was that? I couldn't hear you."

Keep your eyes locked on his. Sure, an easy enough demand for her brain to make. But darn her perfect sight that included twenty-twenty peripheral vision, meaning she could still see the sculpted chest and abs, the tan, tight skin, the patch of chest hair that tapered down between a perfect V of lower abdominal muscles to…

She cleared her throat. "Um, I was just wondering if you needed anything?"

He pointed to his chest, and she hated that her hungry libido followed orders and dipped her gaze.

"A shirt? These pants fit perfectly, though. You keep spare Christmas pj's for all your guests?" he teased. His brows raised in jest, his smile was crooked and…waaaay too adorable. That was to say nothing of the rest of him that looked carved from the same basalt walls as Hurricane Ridge.

"A shirt. Of course. Sorry. Yeah, lemme find one."

"And sorry I took so long in the shower. I guess

I didn't realize how gross I was and the damned cut wouldn't stop bleeding. I tried to stop it, but it's a pretty big gash."

"No worries. I'll grab the shirt, then we'll get to fixing you up."

Heat flashed her skin. Could she say any more embarrassing things? Before she could find out, she spun on her heel so fast, he must have thought she was on fire. Once she was out of sight, she exhaled.

Oh no. What was she thinking, bringing the one man who might be able to do something about Henry's osteogenesis imperfecta into her home? And then lusting after him like a sex-starved young adult? It was unconscionable.

You are *sex-starved. What's it been, three years?*

If her snarky intrusive thoughts were a person, Casey would have slapped them and left the room. Too bad they weren't wrong. And to make matters worse, they followed her wherever she went.

Which, at this moment, was her closet. She'd incorrectly ordered an extralarge T-shirt for a band she'd wanted to see in Scottsdale and had used it as a sleep shirt ever since.

Even though she'd worn the shirt the night before, it smelled clean, so she folded it nicely, grabbed her suture kit and took a deep breath before she went back in the room. She could do this; she was a nurse practitioner, had an advanced degree, was a single mom *and* had buried a husband.

Surely she could be around a handsome man without losing her faculties?

But a handsome man you need in order to help heal your son? What about that?

That sobered her up. She had to remember why she'd taken this job in the first place. It was Ian Matthews who had brought her here, but not for the reasons she'd just daydreamed about.

He was the best mind in the country for treating osteogenesis imperfecta. And Henry, the sweetest boy who'd ever walked the planet, who always reached for her hand when they crossed the street and who stepped over ants so he didn't squish them…that boy deserved the best.

"Here you go," she said, coming around the corner. She stopped in her tracks at the vision reflected from her guest bathroom mirror. Ian was bent over his leg, examining the cut.

"Good grief. You could make it easy on me," she mumbled to herself. Ian was, indeed, a specimen to behold, from his sandy blond hair that resembled a surfer's from Hawaii, to his crystalline blue eyes that reminded her of the glacial pools at the top of the pass she'd flown over on her way in, to his corded muscles that appeared sculpted from nature itself, to…yes, she thought with cheap appreciation, his fine backside.

She might be a widow, but she was apparently very much still alive in that department.

"You say something?" he asked.

"Nope," she replied, setting out the kit and patting the seat she'd dragged from the desk. *Nothing I want you to hear.*

She did have something to say to him, but she wasn't sure how to bring it up. She didn't want to snowball him, especially when she was the one in a position of power in their current situation. She had the needle and thread, she was on home turf and she held all the information.

Ian sat and met her gaze. She held it a beat longer than necessary, then dipped hers to his wound. He'd done a good job cleaning it out.

"This looks good. Are you ready?"

He nodded and set his jaw. *C'mon.* He had to have a square, chiseled jaw, too? Why couldn't the doctor she'd sought out on behalf of Henry be frumpy and boring, instead of attractive, spirited and intense when it came to the way he looked at her—like he actually wanted to figure her out?

"Here we go." She placed a blue surgical napkin across his leg, noting how strong his thighs were before getting back on task. "I'm going to ask you to hold this here, okay?" she asked.

"I can do that. I can also assist if you need."

She threaded the needle while staring at him with a look she hoped would read as how annoying it was to be treated as less-than because of…well, her status as an NP or woman. Or both.

"I'm good, thanks. Do you have any allergies? I'm going to administer a broad range antibiotic and a local anesthetic. Oh, and are you up-to-date on your tetanus?" she asked.

He gave a sharp nod of his head. "I'm fine. I don't need all that. Thanks, though." He sat back, his hand keeping the napkin in place while she put on a headlamp.

She crossed her arms over her chest. If she could project annoyance, she would throw a whole heap of it in his lap. All the degrees and experience and he was just like any other hotshot mountaineer coming in, trying to act brave.

"Let's get one thing straight. You're an amazing doctor with a stellar reputation for saving patients. But if you think this is the way to impress me, you're sorely mistaken. A local anesthetic will help your muscles relax so I can do my job better. The antibiotics will ensure that the wound doesn't get infected, reducing your healing time as well as the risk that you'll need further intervention. And the tetanus—which you don't need?" she confirmed. He shook his head.

"Got it last year," he grumbled.

"Good. So, will you let me do my job?"

"Yes. Sorry." He bowed his head, properly chastised. She felt bad, but not bad enough she regretted her speech. She was a competent nurse and hotshot patients pretending to be impervious to pain frustrated her.

"Thank you. It might sting." She lifted the first needle, the anesthetic, and he turned away. When she brought the sharp point to his leg, he winced before it even pierced his skin. She glanced down at the crescent-shaped marks in his palms and realized it had nothing to do with being a hotshot. He didn't like needles.

Empathy washed away the frustration from before.

Okay, Case. No more assumptions. If you're doing your best, you'd ask questions and leave room for more than one answer. Do better.

"You okay?" she asked.

He nodded. "Talk to me while you work," he said. The casual demand crept underneath her skin and sent a racing chill up her spine. "I… I know it's silly, but I hate needles. Talking distracts me."

The unexpected vulnerability turned the chill to heat, wild and burning. "What do you want to talk about?" she asked. She couldn't for the life of her think of what to say to a man she'd just met who was in her home while she sewed his leg shut, a man she needed in a professional setting and clearly was attracted to in a casual, physical way.

"Anything." She placed the back half of a stitch, and he hissed out a breath. "Do you have a family?" he asked. "A husband? Kids? Greg said something about a son, but does he have siblings?"

He nodded to the room across the way—Henry's. There were toys everywhere. God love her son, but he was a mess like his father had been.

Anything but that…

He must've noticed the way her body froze under this line of questioning.

"Sorry. That was personal. I'm just trying to think of anything but the needle in my leg." As he said that, she placed the second stitch. "You're good at this," he muttered through gritted teeth. "Wish that made it hurt less."

She smiled weakly. "I had a husband," she said. "He passed away two years ago."

"Oh, I'm sorry." He put his other hand on her leg, in the same place as his was on his own leg. "That's the worst."

"It was." She nodded and continued. "And I have a son. Henry." Before her brain could catch up to what she was doing, she added, "He has osteogenesis imperfecta."

She met his gaze as she pulled the thread tight.

"I know you," he whispered. "I mean, I recognize Henry's name and the case. You tried to get him in as a new patient two years ago in Chicago." She nodded. "I quit though—I never went back." She shook her head.

This is it, she thought. *I'm going to be fired.*

Instead, Ian squeezed her leg.

"Okay, then. You've got at least three stitches to go. Tell me about Henry."

CHAPTER THREE

"WHAT DO YOU THINK?" Casey asked him. Thank goodness she'd pointed at the wound and wasn't referring to the conversation they'd just had.

Ian inspected the sutured cut. Casey was damn good at what she did. The best stitch job he'd seen, and with the most gentle touch and bedside manner.

"It's perfect," he told her. "I'll have to thank Greg for insisting on this—there won't even be a scar. Where'd you go to school?"

He recalled something about Arizona, but not a specific location. They'd looked at four applications over the eight months for the position, and he'd been in and out of the clinic during that time.

"University of Arizona in Tucson. I practiced there, too, in Desert Memorial Hospital."

"Well, thanks to them, too. You must have had good teachers."

She shrugged and her cheeks reddened. He didn't push it, after seeing her body's visceral reaction to his quip. He was curious, though. Even though he had no right to be.

Too bad he couldn't keep his head straight and focus on the only reason he was there, in her home—medical intervention.

How could he, when two things were distracting him from rational thought?

First, her news. Casey had come to work at the Hector Ruiz Clinic for him. Not to work alongside him as an osteo surgeon, not because she wanted to learn from how he treated the unique breaks and injuries that came in off the mountain and Salish Sea.

Not even because she harbored a secret crush on him or something like that.

All of those could have been explained away with maybe no more than a raised brow. They wouldn't be deal-breakers that could derail the clinic.

But Casey had uprooted her whole life—her son's whole life—to bring Henry to Ian, who didn't practice that kind of medicine anymore. Wouldn't practice that kind of medicine ever again. And he'd known what that meant for the patients like Henry he'd had to cancel on, knew that his guilt over losing his patient to an unforeseen clot meant he'd worry every time a child was on his table. But what couldn't he see? What was beyond his control that could derail his expertise?

Those questions were why he left. To confront the unknown and hopefully find his way back to medicine.

He almost hadn't come back at all. Greg and Ethan had convinced him to leave Switzerland and come home to do the Olympic hike with them, and that had catapulted him back into the world of medicine when they'd come across Reese and Erin stranded after a helicopter crash.

He was glad to be back, but he wasn't the same man, the same doctor who'd left.

How could he tell her that without changing her whole perception of him? Without nullifying the sacrifices she'd made?

"I know it's crazy that I made the move, but with you not taking patients outside the clinic area, it was the only way I saw to take care of Henry after waiting more than two years for help. I had to take the risk," she said, wiping up the wound with antiseptic and lining up a bandage. "Besides, we were ready for a change. The Pacific Northwest is good for us."

"I understand." He did, too—all of it. That was the thing. He'd have moved to Antarctica if it would have saved his sister. But that wasn't his fate. She'd died because a doctor hadn't been willing to do whatever it took to save her—thus shaping Ian and Greg's choices to become surgeons themselves.

It also shaped his risk-taking in accepting medical cases that others deemed lost causes. And that hadn't worked for him, either. A patient had died because of a heart condition—a ruptured blood vessel no one had seen coming. It was outside of Ian's control, nothing he could have seen or prevented. That was life, but it made him reassess what risks he was willing to take. The stakes were too high, he'd realized that day. His guilt had manifested into demons that made him far more conservative in surgery.

If he could find the courage to tell Casey that, what would she think? That she'd made a mistake, to be sure.

Either way, she was here now, was working with him for the foreseeable future, and he had nothing to offer her. Best he keep his past to himself and hope she wouldn't leave and take her skills—skills the clinic needed—with her because two and a half years ago he'd let the evil brothers Guilt and Grief make his decisions for him.

Because she'd chosen the wrong doctor, the wrong champion.

Dammit. He'd hoped his move to Hoodsport would be a clean start, but it seemed his and Greg's dad was right—wherever he went, there he was. He couldn't hide from his past any more in the woods and canyons than he could in the anonymity of the big city.

"So, what do you think? Do you hate me?"

This time, she wasn't talking about the suture. He shook his head. What would his brother and Reese have to say about this situation? If he screwed this up, they wouldn't ever forgive him. Not when they'd had this search open for eight months before finding someone with Casey's résumé willing to relocate to the middle of nowhere.

Basically, a unicorn.

"Of course not. You did what you had to do to protect your son and I respect that. Besides, we got a pretty amazing nurse practitioner in the deal, so I think we're square."

She bit her bottom lip, and her chin fell even as her gaze still met his. Geez. Did she have any idea how alluring she was?

He hoped not. Which brought him to the second thing distracting him. He'd asked to hear more about Henry to keep him focused, but it wasn't the pain he needed to forget about. Sure, he had a little fear of needles, but he'd endured worse.

What made him wince? Every damn time she leaned in to make another stitch, he caught a whiff of her hair and it bowled him over. What was it? Shampoo? One of those fancy conditioners women used once they were out of the shower?

It was amazing, whatever had caused it. The scent was floral—the same one that had distracted him in the truck. Only this time, he couldn't escape it with an open window. The woman was literally sewing him back together, meaning he was a captive victim to not just the scent, but his body's reaction to it.

Namely, half an erection he could barely hide with the thin holiday pants she'd loaned him.

All he could do was hold his breath and hope that on top of everything else, his body didn't decide this was the woman it wanted to break his two years' worth of celibacy for. He was happy to be back to medicine—and hopefully soon, sex with consenting women who knew he didn't want anything more. But that didn't mean inviting anything resembling romance into his life was a way to live stress-free. As it was, the hiking, climbing and kiteboarding he did in Washington was the ticket to releasing his demons.

Sex with a woman he'd just met, who'd moved there in the hopes he'd treat her son, who worked with him… Yeah, safe to say that was a horrible idea if mitigating stress was the key. And sex with someone with all that baggage, gorgeous or not, was *definitely* off the table.

"Can… Would you be willing to meet him?"

Ian stood. He wanted to sprint out of there, his skin was so itchy. He was too aware of his body, of the temperature in the room—much warmer than he'd been in the forest the past week.

"I don't know. I mean, as the son of a woman I'll be working with, sure. But I can't as a patient. I stopped taking those cases—" He stopped himself.

"A little over two years ago?"

He nodded.

He'd come dangerously close to sharing his greatest regret with her. Not just the loss, but that he hadn't stayed, hadn't worked through it and had let it fester until it affected his ability to practice. He was back, he was ready, and didn't need the scrutiny of anyone other than Greg, who already worried about him. But he couldn't see a child again. He just couldn't.

"Yes. I'm sorry. I know you were hoping for a different answer."

She shrugged, the determined set in her eyes remaining. "Do you mind telling me what happened? I looked for your name all over the country after that and from what I can tell, you dropped off the face of the planet. It was pure luck I saw your face in *Medicine Today* as the spearhead of this cool initiative."

"I did disappear." He didn't offer anything more. What could he say that didn't bare his soul as naked as his body'd been in her shower a few moments prior? "The trauma cases at the clinic are my way back to medicine. I've got no concerns about the kind of work we'll do, but they're all I can take on right now. I'm sorry."

She opened her mouth to say more, but then the front door opened.

"—I told him that and he said his dad told him it's not nice to take a lizard from where he was going, but how did Tommy know where he was going, either?" a kid's voice said.

"Henry?" Casey asked.

"Sorry, love. Henry forgot his stuffy and I told him we could come grab it since you'd be at work. I didn't think you'd be back from picking up that hiker—" a woman said, but she came around the corner and as soon as she saw him, she stopped talking.

"Mom!" Henry ran into her arms.

Casey hugged him and her whole face changed. It was lined with surprise, as if she wasn't expecting the intrusion, but also a joy that could only be described as a mother who loved her kid fiercely. Ian's chest hurt watching the scene.

Especially when she put him down gently on the couch and said, "Be careful, though. Remember that even if I'm there to catch you, if I fell or tripped—"

"I'd break my bones and we'd go to the hospital. I *know*, Mom."

She smiled and Ian took in the boy in front of him. He wasn't very tall for a five-year-old, and his spine had a slight curve to it, as did his legs. But otherwise, he looked like a healthy, loved kid with energy and a sparkle in his eyes.

Henry met his gaze and his eyes widened. Only then did Ian see the slight gray color of the whites of his eyes. His heart lurched. If he hadn't gone through what he had, he'd take on this case, but he couldn't take the risks with another child patient.

Traumas? Yes, absolutely. He had to act quick and without much thought for what could be and instead had to focus on what was right in front of him. But unique cases with infinite possibilities and outcomes—including death or paralysis? He might've had great outcomes in treating those kinds of cases earlier in his career, the kind that had led him to have the kind of career and reputation he'd had for fifteen years, but that kind of success had a dark underbelly.

It led to families seeking him out to care for the kids they loved most. Kids like the one he'd lost on his table. Kids like Henry.

No, thanks. Never again.

"Who are you?" Henry asked.

From the corner of his eye, Ian saw Casey's mom giving him the once-over, likely wondering the same thing.

"I'm Ian Matthews, the doctor at the clinic where your mom started working this week."

"You were hiking in the tornado alley, weren't you?" Henry asked. Ian chuckled.

"Hurricane Ridge, and yep, I was, but I got hurt and your mom was sent to help me."

Henry jumped in the air and Casey flinched beside them. What must it be like to be in constant worry about your child—more so than parents were already? The world was made to harden and break the strongest people and Henry's body wasn't born able to withstand the brunt of childhood, let alone growing up.

"Awesome! Will you take me one day? I'm a good hiker, I promise. Even with my oshear—my osheara…"

"Osteogenesis imperfecta," Casey said. Her smile was sad.

"Yeah," Henry said, "that. But I'm a good hiker and my teacher said there's newts up there that are black and poisonous and I wanna go catch some. Will you take me?"

"Sure," Ian said. His pulse quickened when he glanced at Casey and found her staring at him, an unreadable expression on her face. "I also know a dozen places you can find those newts around here. We can definitely go look sometime if your mom says it's okay."

Casey cleared her throat. "Sure."

Her mom came over and stuck out a hand. "I'm Brenda, Casey's mom. It's nice to meet you, Ian. Now, why don't we let your mom finish up here. Go grab Mr. Octopus and we'll get out of here."

She winked at Casey, a gesture that wasn't lost on Ian. He swallowed a chuckle.

"Nice to meet you, too."

"Mr. Octopus is a Great Pacific octopus," Henry said as his grandmother ushered him back to his room. "My mom said we're gonna go see some this summer and you can come with us if you want."

"Thanks, Henry," Ian said, smiling more broadly than he had in a long time. "They're cool animals and are some of the smartest creatures on the planet."

He jumped again, his fist pounding in the air. "I know, right? Mom says they're like me. All jelly and brains."

He looked over at Casey, who was beet red. "She's right."

"Okay, buddy, I'll come help you grab him."

"Can we stay with you guys?" Henry asked. Casey's smile fell.

"You have to stay with grandma since I work early," she said. "Just like in Arizona."

"Okay, Mom," he said, shrugging.

A few minutes later, Henry hugged his mom goodbye, and she shut the door behind him. She told Ian she was going to change into more comfortable clothes and left him alone with his thoughts.

Largely, they were about Henry, about what a cool kid he was. A lot of OI kids he'd treated walked around as if the world was out to get them, but Henry was different. He had a fighter's spirit, even if his body would struggle to catch up.

You know, with a positive attitude like he has, you could—

No. He shut down the infinitesimal part of him that craved solving complex problems like the one Henry's condition created. That only opened the door to unforeseen challenges and bad outcomes. Better to let the kid live a good life with some limitations than no life at all, in search of something more that might never come to pass.

Ian took the opportunity to peruse the living room. Along the staircase wall there were a dozen photos in different colored frames made of different materials. Tans and sea greens were alongside black and silver, wood and metal. The collage was classy and added a splash of personality to the otherwise beige space. It wasn't like the home wasn't decorated beautifully, but aside from the photos, it seemed benign. Safe.

Inside the frames were photos of Casey and Henry at various ages. When he was an infant, wrapped in a blanket on the beach with Casey in a modest swimsuit that still made Ian's throat dry. She was a beautiful woman at every age and stage. Some photos had caught her laughing, Henry nuzzled by her side in most of them. Ian fought back a stab of jealousy at whoever had the intimate access to Casey to draw out that easy smile from her.

Other photos had Casey's mom in them, and one, in the center, was a photo taken from behind its subjects at the Grand Canyon. Casey's blond hair made it easy to discern that it was her and Henry, but there was a man's arm wrapped around them both.

That must be the husband she'd mentioned. The one who'd died.

Why weren't there more photos of him? Ian wondered. He'd never been close enough to a romantic partner to consider building a life with them, raising children together, but if he ever got there, and something happened to them?

He'd be devastated.

Ian shivered even though the home's thermostat must be set at seventy-two. Fear of losing someone he loved was part of why he didn't date much at all in the first place. His brother, Greg, was the opposite. As a serial monogamist, he was always searching for "the one," thinking that would fill the gap made when their sister was taken from them way too soon when she'd gone in for a routine appendectomy and never left the hospital. The doctor had noticed a bleed but written in his notes that he expected it to close on its own; that hadn't happened. His sister had bled out before the night was over. What had she been? Twelve? All he remembered about the day of her surgery was fighting over why she got the bigger room and telling her he'd take the room for himself if she died. What an asshole of an eight-year-old little brother he'd been.

Because she did die. And he'd thought he'd caused that with his wish to have her bedroom with the hardwood floors that he could build Legos on. She'd missed her first kiss, her first trip on an airplane, her first class on a university campus. Or maybe she'd have traveled instead of going to college, run away with a high school boyfriend to Spain or Alaska or something.

They wouldn't ever know. They wouldn't ever get to know her struggles and joys and hopes and fears, things a family should know. And because of that, caring for someone else other than Greg was one risk Ian wasn't ever comfortable taking.

Ian couldn't understand how a risk-averse man like Greg couldn't see that love was far riskier than the occasional cliff jump, rock climb or even kite-surfing on Puget Sound.

At least if Ian fell off a cliff or slipped like he had earlier today, he'd only injure his body, and it would heal. His heart? Well, he couldn't see how a metaphysical organ could cause so much pain. He was the same broken person he'd been when his parents returned from the hospital alone, faces tear-streaked and emotionally gutted.

Hell, they all were. None of them had recovered. So no, he wouldn't be inviting anyone into his heart. Especially not someone with a son who reminded him of the part of his profession he'd left behind.

Casey came back a few minutes later, dressed in a floral tank top and pale blue sleep pants that highlighted her eyes. Her hair was down and fell over her shoulders.

Wow. When he'd met her, he'd been attracted to her simple, elegant style, at the way she carried herself, even if it was a little stiff for his tastes. When he'd discovered why—she was balancing a lot as a widow and single parent to an OI child—he'd been more than interested.

He was impressed.

Now, another emotion hit him from behind his heart, where he'd just confirmed it was locked away and quiet.

Admiration. That was *way* worse than thinking she was beautiful.

She poured herself a mug of tea from a kettle in the kitchen and asked if he wanted one. He accepted only because he wasn't ready to go to bed yet. For some dumb reason, completely counter to his earlier self-admonition to keep Casey at arm's length because he didn't need anything resembling romantic entanglement, he wanted the night to continue.

It's because I'm going to be working closely with her at the clinic. I should get to know her better.

Sure, his conscience chimed in. *That checks out.*

He ignored the sarcastic chuckle from the part of him that knew his antics best.

When she handed him his mug of tea, her thumb brushed his. The heat wasn't from the cup of liquid but warmed him, still.

"Thanks for earlier. For what you did for Henry. You were good with him. Had I known she was bringing him by, I never would have—"

"Stop," he said. "It's fine. I know it wasn't an ambush." He'd seen the shock in her eyes, coupled with the love that followed. "And from what I've seen, you're an amazing mother, Casey. There's no faulting what you'd do to protect your son. He's a neat kid."

She sat down and sipped her tea, smiling. He loved how she blossomed when he mentioned Henry. It made him want to keep asking about the boy, if only to keep that grin on her face.

"Yeah, he is. The octopus thing is a joke between

us. When we were reading about animals one night, he was sad he'd never get to climb like a monkey or run like a cheetah. I told him that was fine—land animals were boring anyway. He was like an octopus, which is as smart as a monkey and can fit in tinier spaces."

"Plus, their bodies can change to match their environments," Ian added. "And they've been known to be jokesters in aquariums."

Casey laughed, almost spilling her tea. "Shoot. But yeah, you're right. I'll tell him that, too."

They sat in silence for a minute and she fiddled with her mug. He really didn't want the evening to end. It was…nice to sit in gentle, quiet comfort with a person he kinda liked talking to.

But what could he do? He was a guest in her home.

When she stood up, he went to do the same and tried to hide his disappointment.

"Oh no, don't get up. I was just gonna…" She pointed to the remote on the coffee table. "Do you want to watch a movie? I started a new rom-com but I'm only five minutes in. I'm just not tired yet. I rarely get—"

"Time off from being a mom?"

She nodded, her cheeks the same pink as they'd been at the parking lot.

"Is that awful?"

He shook his head and patted the couch next to him. "Not at all. You were a person with needs before you became a mom. Taking care of yourself is the only way you can show up for Henry fully, too."

"Pretty smart," she said. When she sat next to him, he was pleased to note she sat closer to him this time. He shut down his sarcastic subconscious from commenting. There'd be time for that. "You must be a doctor or something."

He laughed. "Or something. Anyway, tell me about this movie. I'll admit I haven't seen any movies or TV lately."

She spoke about the plot and he watched with awe as she gesticulated and laughed about how the actors had worked together on another project and might have had a little romantic thing in real life. He liked when Casey talked. He'd had the initial impression she was stoic, maybe a little stuck-up. But that was proving to be anything but the truth.

She restarted the movie and they got through half an hour of the thing, her laughing so hard she snorted at one point. He tried to keep his composure, but it was infectious and he joined in the silliness of the romantic comedy. It wasn't his genre, but if it got her this happy, maybe he could get into it.

She would be fun to work with, he decided. He was looking forward to going back to the clinic Monday. Hell, his leg didn't really hurt anymore. This distraction was just what he needed.

When she didn't giggle at the main character's slipup, he glanced over. She was asleep, a peaceful smile on her face. To make matters worse, she was leaning on his shoulder—or rather, on a throw pillow that was propped on his shoulder. Her long hair cascaded across the pillow and his arm and when he inhaled, there was that floral scent again.

Damn. His body calmed at the same time he got hyperaware. It was kinda like being on the precipice of a ravine or just before a major surgery. He'd never experienced it with…

With a woman? Someone you kind of like?

How could he like her? He didn't know her at all.

Yeah, but you wanna. Good grief. Time to shut down that snarky inner critic.

He put a hand on her shoulder, rousing her gently.

"Casey?" She purred and smiled, her eyes still heavy with sleep.

"Do you wanna go to bed?"

She shook her head and slid down his arm until her head landed in his lap.

"Here. Just…here. One minute."

Well, crap. What was he supposed to do now? Leave her there? He brushed off the hair that had fallen across her cheek.

She stretched and he ignored the way her sleep shirt had crept up her stomach, exposing her taut, smooth skin. No, he couldn't, in good conscience, let her lie on a stranger's lap no matter how comforting it was to him. *And yeah,* he told the voice that had gone eerily quiet in his head, *I'll investigate my feelings on that later.*

"Hey, Casey, I'm gonna head to bed." He rubbed her shoulder.

She sat up with a start and he bit back a smile. Her hair was wild and with a hint of curl now that it was mussed up. He had to be honest—it looked a heck of a lot better than it did all straight and neat.

What would the rest of her look like if she let go? Let things get wild instead of tame and safe?

He allowed his imagination to go so far as to picture her on a ridge with him, dirt on her shoulders and legs, a smile on her face. But he stopped short at thinking of her at home, letting loose while he was there…

Nope. Not going there.

"Did I fall asleep?" she asked. He nodded.

"Yep. Looks like you got too cozy on that throw pillow." He pointed at the pillow that had migrated to his lap, and she gasped.

"Oh no. I… I put that—" She gestured. He shook his head, sensing her embarrassment and wanting to shut it down for her.

"No. You started on my shoulder." That somehow made it worse. He grimaced. "It's okay, you didn't do anything wrong, Casey."

"And then I lay on—" She touched his lap, then recoiled.

He nodded again. "It's fine, though. I didn't mind. You looked peaceful."

She shook her head and stood. "Still, that's ridiculous. I must have been exhausted, but it's no excuse. It's so unprofessional. I'm sorry, Ian. For asking about Henry, for falling asleep on you..." She paused and shifted her feet. "I'm not normally like this. So all over the place."

He got up and pulled her into an embrace. He couldn't say why he felt the need to—only that it seemed like the right thing to do.

"You're fine, Casey. Better than fine. Thanks for taking care of me tonight, from picking me up, to suturing my wound, to letting me in your space. It'll be nice working with someone I enjoy and respect already, and I can't tell you how long it's been since I just sat on a couch and watched a movie."

"Well, I still feel guilty. I practically accosted you, after telling you I moved here so you could help me treat my son. You must think I'm nuts."

Pretty, kind and caring, sure. But not nuts. "No," he said instead. "I don't. I think you care about your kid and I'm sorry I'm not that doc anymore."

"Me, too," she whispered. She walked back to her bedroom and stopped at the doorway. "I know you, you know," she said. She paused and let him read into that. "I researched you—your life and the cases you took on that made the headlines. You loved that kind of medicine. I hope one day you'll find your way back to it, and not because of Henry or kids like him who need a doctor like you. But because in every news story, the way you were photographed looking at your patients as if they were something special? Yeah, you can't teach that. You were born to do what you left behind in Chicago and that kind of passion doesn't just fade away with time." She glanced down the hallway toward Henry's room. "Trust me."

With that, she left him with more questions than answers. The biggest one of all was why his chest and heart hurt more than the newly sutured wound on his leg.

Only second to that was just when had he made a mistake—because at this point, it felt more and more like he had.

Was it in leaving medicine altogether and adventuring in Switzerland's peaks and valleys? Or was it in moving here, where his mistakes and fears and dreams all butted up against one another and with mountains or deep seas on each side, there was no place to go.

Like it or not, he was minutes away from a reckoning where he'd come face-to-face with every single thing he'd avoided for years.

Why did he feel like Casey Larsen would be at the center of it all?

CHAPTER FOUR

THE NEXT DAY, Casey awoke and put on her tights, an oversized angora wool sweater and her Cascadia boots, and tucked her hair in a ball cap advertising the Seattle Kraken, the local hockey team.

Dressed, she sighed and made a list of what she'd need to do before she picked up Henry at her mom's.

She'd drop Ian off at his truck and then walk through the Community Trail Park.

She'd need to grab groceries before Henry got home, or he'd want half the junk food aisle and she was powerless to deny that kind of treat to him.

Her stomach rumbled and she realized the last thing she'd eaten was a burger from O'Connor's. That triggered a few other memories from the night before, memories she was trying to shove down where they couldn't embarrass her anymore.

She'd told Ian about taking the NP position so she could work with him.

Then she'd told him why just as Henry had shown up, forcing Ian's hand in meeting him.

And adding insult to injury, she'd fallen asleep on his lap, like he was a date she'd invited over, rather than the patient-slash-colleague-slash-stranger he really was.

Good gracious, she really knew how to make an entrance into a new town and job, didn't she?

The thing was, he'd handled all of it with grace. Somehow, that only added to the awkwardness she felt now, facing him in the light of a new day.

The low hum of his deep voice came from the other side of her bedroom door. It sent a shiver up her spine. She figured he'd be connecting with Greg, his brother, or one of the other docs. She'd met all those doctors in the interview process, so she'd known what to expect coming here to work with them.

Erin was sweet and yet the strongest woman Casey'd ever met. She was a great mom to Reese's daughter, Libby, too. Reese was talented and like her, from the city, only a wetter one than her past life. He'd be the one to show her the ropes out here and help her acclimate to the rural wilderness. He and Erin made a darling couple.

Greg, Ian's brother, was polished and put together, handsome in the conventional sense and—now that she'd met Ian, she could say this with confidence—his brother's polar opposite. Where Greg was polished, Ian had a rough, wild edge to him. Where Greg brought the conversation back to safety, Ian had just been sutured up for taking big risks.

Where Greg held no allure to her other than as a responsible colleague she couldn't wait to work with, Ian got under her skin and made parts of her awaken—parts that had been dormant for years.

And now she had to share not only the day with him, but each day going forward. Maybe she'd luck out and be paired on shifts with one of the other docs.

Sure, because you're totally that lucky.

"Better get this over with," she muttered.

As soon as she opened the door, she was met with the scent of eggs and butter. And…coffee?

Her stomach roared with delight.

"Hey, there. I hope you don't mind, but I snooped in your fridge and there wasn't much, so I walked down to the Red Hen and got us some food. Sandwiches and to-go lattes in case you planned on eating in the car."

"Um, thanks," she said, taking the paper cup from him. She inhaled and almost swooned. "Vanilla?" she asked.

"Yep. Saw the vanilla creamer in your fridge and took a guess. Hope it's okay?"

She nodded as that part of her she'd been keeping an eye on since she woke up in Ian's lap the night before stretched and yawned… The part of her heart that longed to be taken care of after being the one to take care of everyone, Lawrence included when he'd checked out from a parental role after Henry's diagnosis. The part of her that just wanted a partner who noticed the little things.

No. Not this guy, not this time. We're here to work and take care of Henry.

Besides, she could accept a thoughtful gesture from a man without it meaning anything more, right?

"Thanks again. It was really nice of you and wholly unnecessary."

"Nonsense," he said, slinging his backpack over his shoulder as if it weighed nothing. "It's the least I can do after you sutured my leg. Anyway, I'm sure you're busy. Should we head out?"

"Sounds good. Lemme just get my bag."

They were driving when Greg called. Ian put him on Speaker.

"Hey, can you pick up Scout this morning? The shop has to close and I'm not back till tonight. Oh, and how's the leg?"

"Leg's fine. Thanks for setting that up. I'm actually with Casey right now, heading back to get my truck. But who's Scout again?"

There was silence on the other end. "Scout is the dog I told you about. But, um, you wanna take me off Speaker, bro?"

Casey pulled over to the shoulder in case plans were changing. Ian's cheeks flashed with red, but he took his brother off Speaker. The cab was so quiet that she could still hear Greg through Ian's speaker.

"Dude, you didn't—"

"No," Ian said, cutting him off and tossing Casey a look. *Sorry*, he mouthed. She shook her head. "Nothing like that. I couldn't drive so she took me to her house since it was closer."

"Why didn't you head to the clinic?" Greg asked.

"You texted me that it was shut down for the night. Anyway, we can get into this later. What do you need with Scout?"

"Oh, can you grab him at Bark and Treat? I don't trust him in my house with the new furniture."

Casey winced. "We can get him right now," she suggested. It was on the way to the trail parking lot and otherwise out of Ian's way.

You sure? he mimed. She nodded even though the idea of a dog in her new truck terrified her.

"Yeah," Ian said. "We'll handle it. You owe me," he added.

"Sure," Greg said, and hung up.

They picked up the young dog, which was the most darling thing she'd ever seen aside from her son. A sleek brindle coat wrapped around the energetic animal who couldn't stop wagging his tail and giving them both kisses.

"Well, hell," Ian said, putting him on the floor at his feet. "I was hoping he'd be an ugly SOB but he's kinda cute, isn't he?"

"He's the best boy," Casey said, reaching around and petting him. "How old is he?"

Ian shrugged. "I dunno. Maybe two? Greg said he's a rescue, but young."

"Well, he's adorable." Maybe she and Henry would get a small dog themselves, something Henry could love, but that wouldn't bowl him over and injure him.

In seconds, Scout was asleep at Ian's feet, lightly snoring.

They drove to the lot, talking about Henry's antics with harboring horny toads in his old bedroom in Tucson, and how he was liking the Pacific Northwest. Ian told her about the clinic from his perspective—how it had reignited all the things he'd loved about medicine: the excitement, the feeling that every day would be different, and how it gave back to a community that needed it. The way he described it, the clinic had brought him out of retirement and into a place where he loved practicing again. She had so many questions about that, but there would be time. They were colleagues now.

Maybe even one day they would be friends. Her skin tingled with that possibility, but it competed with another, larger one. She'd moved out here to get help for Henry and couldn't imagine that particular possibility was gone. Ian was still practicing, so there was still hope. She would wait and feel him out and maybe use the time to ask him about other options for Henry. How to do that without pushing too much, too fast, was the delicate balance she'd yet to find. But why was she supposed to care about balance when Henry's quality of life hung in the balance?

It felt like when she used to walk along a cliffside—like she skirted something dangerous—but that was motherhood. And every day of Henry's life. She could be brave, too.

It was easy conversation, even the silences between topics. When they pulled up to his truck, she found herself a little bummed. Sure, they had time to get to know one another, but that didn't mean she wanted today to end, either.

"Thanks again," he told her. His hand was on the door handle and she couldn't help but wonder if he felt the same—that he'd felt their connection and enjoyed her company, too. "I had a great time, all things considered. I think this was a good test for how you'll handle the stress of the clinic."

She frowned. Okay, so maybe he was less excited by her and more by what he wanted out of a nurse practitioner.

"How's that?"

"Well, you were okay with picking up a stranger in the middle of nowhere and bringing him to a safe, sterile location to suture him up." He paused and she tried not to stare at him, open-mouthed. "I'm kidding," he finally said.

"Oh?" She released a breath.

"I mean, your résumé spoke for you, or we

wouldn't have hired you. That you didn't so much as flinch when I brought my dirty self off the trail speaks to you as a person more than as a nurse." He chewed the inside of his lip. Was he nervous? "I'm fumbling this. I only meant to say this was a strange way to meet you—and Henry. But I'm glad I did outside of the clinic."

She shouldn't have felt as good about that as she did—what did his words matter to her apart from knowing she was practicing good medicine? But warmth flooded her stomach and she couldn't hold her smile from blossoming.

"Thanks. Me, too."

"Well," he said. "See you at the office?"

She nodded. "Keep me posted on your injury," she added.

"You bet."

There was a small pause before he opened the door, but neither of them filled it. Unfortunately, they wouldn't get the chance. As soon as there was enough of a gap, Scout startled awake and bolted out of the truck.

"Dammit," Ian said, taking off after him.

She was glad she'd worn her athletic gear as she too jumped out of the truck and chased the two down a dirt path different from the one Ian had come up the day before.

"Scout," they both shouted. But the dog was indifferent to their calls. He ran like an animal possessed, barking at something she couldn't see. As she rounded a corner, she almost collided with Ian's backside. Scout was sitting at his side, tongue out and calm as if he'd done his duty and was fine settling down. He stared up at the cliffside.

"What's he doing?" she wondered aloud.

"Check it out," Ian said, making his way up a small path in the line of sight of where Scout stared. A bike tire stuck out over the outlook, barely visible from the main path.

"Is that a—" she asked.

"Shhh," he said, putting a hand on her shoulder. It felt like the sun hit her there, even though she wore a long-sleeved sweater. "Listen."

She honed her focus and sure enough, heard a whimper from above them where the tire lay.

They didn't need to say a thing to one another. Scout tore off up a little game path and they followed him. Finally, they reached a ledge that was nearly thirty feet above the trail they'd taken to find the dog. A mountain bike lay on its side covered in mud, and behind it, tucked against the cliff edge, was its rider, who looked like he was in bad shape.

His leg was bent at an angle that suggested multiple fractures. A glance above showed he'd probably fallen a good twenty feet, meaning possible internal bleeding as well.

"Good boy," Ian said, petting Scout. The dog lay down behind the rider as Ian moved the bike, giving them better access to assess for injuries.

"I can't believe he heard that from the truck,"

Casey said. Scout just leaned his head on the biker's uninjured leg. "What a good boy, Scout. You did a good thing, bringing us here."

"I was gonna give Greg grief for adopting a dog, but this guy's earned his stripes on day one. I owe him a steak when we make it back."

Ian stabilized the patient's neck with his sweatshirt, which he'd tugged off, revealing a tight grey wool shirt underneath. Casey concentrated on finding the mountain biker's pulse, but out of the corner of her eye, she acknowledged Ian's frame. He was strong, but it wasn't the kind of strength that came from barbells or machines. This guy looked as if he was formed from the cliffs and peaks she'd admired since touching down in Washington. Thank goodness, too. Their accidental patient would need to be carried out of here, and they didn't have time to wait for emergency medical services.

"His pulse is thready," Casey reported. Ian leaned down and put an ear to the patient's chest. His skin was pale and clammy.

"Breathing, too. Weak on the right side. Likely a bleed."

"His leg will need help, too," she added. "What's the plan?" She hadn't come prepared with more than a basic first aid kit in her truck. She glanced at her cell phone and noted that she didn't have much in the way of service, either.

"I've got a sat phone in the truck, and a fully

stocked med kit in my pack. Do you feel comfortable if I go back?"

"Of course." Casey made a note to get a better kit of her own for the truck when she had her next day off. This was too rugged an area to get away with her measly antiseptic cream and bandages. She'd need compresses, sutures, splints and tubing most likely.

She sat with the man and talked to him for a few minutes but if he knew she was there, he gave no indication. All the while, Scout stayed by his side. The man moaned and Scout nuzzled closer to his legs.

"Can you hear me?" Casey asked. "My name is Casey and I'm a nurse practitioner. We're here to help."

The man's eyes shot open and he hissed in a breath. It sounded like a whistle and Casey took his hand gently. This was going to hurt now that the man was conscious. Sure enough, his eyes watered and he groaned.

"I—" he tried, but pain must have rocketed through him because he cried out and almost lost consciousness again. He glanced down at his leg and his eyes got wide. From his knee down, the bone wasn't facing the direction it should.

"It's okay. You don't have to talk. You've fallen off a pretty big cliff and likely injured some things beside your leg. We're going to take care of you in Hoodsport once we make sure you can travel.

Again, my name is Casey. I'm a nurse. Ian will be back in a minute and he's an orthopedic surgeon. You're in good hands, okay?"

"Casey," he whispered. She nodded. He lifted a shaky finger and pointed at his chest. Even through his white shirt, she could see bruising discoloration creeping up his right side. "Jeff."

"Hi, Jeff. I'm sorry you're in so much pain, but we're going to make sure you're okay, alright?"

He gave a small nod, barely perceptible. He tried to squeeze her hand, but his grip was weak.

"Rachel."

Casey frowned. "Is Rachel your wife?"

Another curt nod followed by a hiss of pain.

Dang it. Did they have a second patient out there?

"Is she with you?" Instead of a nod, a single shake of his head.

"Home. Kids."

He passed out again and she dug in his bike pack until she found what she was looking for—his phone. It was locked, so she kept digging around until she got to his wallet.

His name was Jeffrey Phillips, according to his driver's license. She tucked the ID back and waited for Ian to get back. What the heck was Jeff doing out there, in dangerous terrain, alone, when he had a family at home? Why not just ride close to civilization?

Because what would have happened if they

weren't there? If Scout hadn't found the rider? What would his kids have done without a dad?

Casey's eyes closed tight as a wave of memories came back to her. She didn't care that people went out and did crazy things and risked their lives for the sake of an adrenaline boost. She understood the need to feel alive and even remembered what she'd loved about scuba diving with her father in the northern part of the Sea of Cortez as a teen and young adult.

It had been thrilling, driving together south from Tucson, the sun on her shoulder as they drove toward the ocean, her first love. She'd always get antsy the closer they got to the border; then when the sea was in view, her little landlocked heart would soar.

When he'd died the year she went to college, part of her had, too. Sure, it brought her and her mother closer together in their shared grief, but it also left a gaping hole where he used to be. Odd that she still felt that hole in her heart, but the one Lawrence had made was filling in—partly because he'd shoveled so much behind him as he'd slowly exited the marriage.

She'd actually met Lawrence on a dive trip, which had been another wonderful adventure of its own. They'd toured the world together for their honeymoon—diving the Red Sea, a bucket list place that had stolen her breath, then on to Hawaii where they'd done a night dive with dozens of manta rays… They'd ended the trip in her favorite place of all, the place that had started it all for her. It had been magical, sharing that special time with her new partner. To her, at least. He'd found it "quaint and cute," but she'd known that Puerto Peñasco and the Sea of Cortez bored him.

Lawrence was all about the thrill, the chase, the danger. That had been sexy at first, but over time, she'd wondered if a full life with all of its seasons would be enough for him. She'd gotten her answer three years after their honeymoon when they found out they were pregnant.

A few months into that adventure, at a routine ultrasound she'd gone to alone since Lawrence was on a rock climbing trip with his college roommate, she'd gotten news that changed the course of her life irrevocably.

Henry, her sweet little boy she hadn't even met yet—wouldn't for six more months—had a rare bone disease that, if it didn't kill him at birth or before, would make life significantly harder for him. And even then, he might not have the same lifespan as other kids. Her heart had shattered that day, not just for her son's health, which was its own type of grief she'd never recover from, but for what it did to her life. To Lawrence's.

That might have been selfish of her, but she couldn't help the feelings that cropped up so suddenly. And the sooner she processed them, the sooner she could get to wrapping her head around her new existence so she could support Lawrence when she told him.

By the time she left the obstetrician's office, she'd come to a definitive conclusion—it would be okay. She'd known what being a parent meant, even if this diagnosis wasn't part of her dreams of raising a child. But none of that mattered anymore. Her one job was to parent the child she was given.

Her husband hadn't ever understood that. In fact, she'd been appalled at how unfazed he was about the whole thing when he'd gotten home from his Colorado climbing expedition.

He'd kissed her forehead while she cried and said the words they'd once said together. "It's fine. Having a kid doesn't change anything—we'll just bring him." He'd added, "We'll just be careful."

He'd kept up his lifestyle, leaving her alone for long periods of time during her pregnancy in which her darker thoughts were given freedom to come out.

Her life would no longer lead her to thrilling adventures that elevated her heart rate for a bit. And likely wouldn't ever again. It would be about keeping her son safe so he could live as long as possible.

No more diving, no more travel, no more hiking up boulders in the foothills of the Catalina Mountains.

She'd need to be the responsible parent.

And she was. According to her mom, she was responsible to a fault. *Look at why,* she wanted to say. *My son has a disease that will impact every decision he makes, from the way he steps off a curb, to the way he plays with friends.*

And I alone will be there to support him as he learns to navigate that.

And she was. She loved it, even if it was hard. Every day was its own adventure with a son who'd barely survived his own birth and had lost his other parent. He needed her.

Lawrence was a different story. Her earlier worries were met with the facts—he needed something else, and the more distance he created between him and the rest of his family, the more she saw that had always been the case; it had just suited her before she'd gotten pregnant. But if she was being honest, Lawrence was only ever about the adventure from the start. He'd liked having her along for them—and to plan them—but anything resembling a mundane or static life had always terrified him. It was actually a wonder that he'd stuck around for Henry's birth at all.

Footsteps combined with labored breathing behind her tore her from the rocky walk down memory lane. She turned to find Ian jogging up the last part of the trail.

Wow, he's beautiful, her mind drummed up. He was, but that wasn't anything she should be noticing, and not only because they had a patient to treat. With his love of the next adventure, the next thrill—obvious in how she'd met him on the trail the day before—Ian was too similar to Lawrence. If she ever opened her heart again—which was a big *if*—she needed a man who understood how fragile her son's life was. She needed an actual partner.

Ian's casual mention that he and her son could go newt-foraging—like it was the easiest, risk-free way to spend an afternoon—showed that even if he was a physician who treated ortho cases like Henry's, he had no idea how to raise a boy with those challenges. She could never risk that he might be as careless and cavalier as Lawrence had been.

"Hey, sorry. I had to dig out the kit but I've got everything we need to get him taken care of here. I made the call to EMS, too."

"Thanks. And no worries. What did EMS say?"

"They'll send a flight out, but we need to find a way to get him safely to the parking lot without doing much damage."

"He passed out again, but before he did, he told me his name is Jeff Phillips and his wife is Rachel. She's home with kids, I think. Did you bring the sat phone so I can call and let her know to meet us at the clinic?"

Ian nodded, then frowned. "I did." He handed her the phone from a pack he'd brought. "I know the trail he was on and it's no joke. Unless he's a professionally sponsored mountain biker, he had no business being out here alone."

Ian's comments echoed hers. Interesting coming

from the man who'd just left a weeklong trip in the backcountry of the Olympics.

"Do you ever worry when you're out there alone?" she asked.

Ian met her gaze. "Yes. But I'm not leaving family behind to worry about me. I'd do things differently if that was the case." He seemed to understand the subtext of what she was asking and she liked his answer. It was different than Lawrence's had been, that was for certain. Guilt at her earlier internal thoughts about his similarities to her late husband nagged at her. Maybe patience was necessary in more than one area where Ian was concerned.

Ian cut off Jeff's biker jersey so they could see what they were dealing with.

"There's bruising along his right lower quadrant."

"Do you think he broke a rib and punctured his right lung?" she asked. If that was the case, it elevated the issues they were dealing with tenfold.

"I do, unfortunately."

"Do we need to put in a chest tube out here in the field?"

Ian chuckled, but it was without humor. "I've only seen that done once, with a water hose from a hiking bladder. Erin did it when they crashed out here."

"So what do you think we need? I've splinted chest injuries like this in the Catalinas when a hiker's path slid out beneath him and a rock crushed his chest. We can use a needle to decompress the tension pneumothorax and then wrap his chest."

"That might work," he said, holding her gaze. "Hmm. I don't know that we have a better option. Lead the charge, Casey."

"Are you sure? You're the orthopedic surgeon."

He nodded. "I am, and I'm also injured."

Her hand flew to her mouth. "I can't believe I just let you run that whole way!"

He smiled. "If it makes you feel any better, I speed-walked and lightly jogged. And between the pain killer you gave me and your expert surgical suturing skills, I flat forgot you did that just yesterday. The sutures also held up the whole path down and back, so you come with rave reviews, Nurse Casey."

She smiled and nodded, grabbing a needle from Ian's fully stocked kit. A rush of adrenaline flooded her bloodstream and she fought a smile of her own. She hadn't felt this…this alive in a long time.

"What is our plan of attack?" she asked. "After his lungs?"

"I'll take care of his leg, but his chest will take priority. Without that, he won't make it to the parking lot. Can you do that?"

She loved being a mom more than anything in the world. Second? She loved her work.

Casey's training and experience kicked into high gear. Lately, she'd taken low-risk jobs in easy-to-work-at hospitals and clinics, places that would allow her to be flexible if she needed to be there for Henry.

And she'd been bored. She was a talented nurse practitioner, had graduated top of her class and had done everything by the book. She'd wanted more than placing IVs and doing research for other physicians and practitioners, but wouldn't trade her life or child for it.

But in that moment, her son safe with her mom, she allowed her true feelings to surface.

She missed the adventure of it all, even if she couldn't have it in her day-to-day life.

"I can," she said, positioning the needle above the second intercostal space. "Let's do this."

She punctured the air pocket in the pleural cavity through the rib cage and heard a hiss of air as the lung inflated. The patient didn't wake up, but his breath sounds regulated and slowly, color came back to his skin.

In the distance, the sound of a chopper cut through the silence of the empty trail.

"They're here. Once we get him to the chopper, we'll bring him to the clinic and I'll fix the rest there."

"Not Seattle?" she asked.

He glanced at the building grey clouds she'd seen on the horizon earlier. They bunched over the mountains now.

"No," he declared. "The clinic is safer with the weather. But Casey?" he asked.

She could barely hear him between the rush of blood to her head and the chopper's blades behind them.

"Yeah?" she called.

"You did great today. Yesterday, too. I'm so damn glad you're my—my colleague." His pause gave her heart a flutter. Was he going to say *friend*?

She never found out. The helicopter dipped and landed in the parking lot. The emergency workers on board came down with a stretcher.

"It's go time. Ready to transport the patient?"

She nodded and they carefully maneuvered Jeff onto the stretcher. They each lifted a side and made their way down the trail, Scout following.

It'd been the strangest month of her life making this move to the Pacific Northwest and settling in before she started work—from the rainy weather, to the abundance of green and living organisms, and now to the type of medicine she would be able to practice.

Her life might be devoid of risk most of the time, but perhaps, just perhaps, there was a way she could infuse a bit more of it into her day-to-day.

For the first time in a long time, Casey Larsen was excited for her future. And, if she did things right, for Henry's, too. Ian was the man, the doctor, he needed—Casey was sure of it. And her job was just the sort of fulfillment she'd desired.

A small part of her rejoiced, but there was a second part—namely her heart—that plummeted, carrying her mood with it. She was attracted to Ian, found him to be an unexpected breath of life in her world. A friend with the pulsing potential for…*more*. She hadn't gone looking for it; more than likely, she'd actively avoided anything like romance.

So color her surprised that she'd found what she hadn't known she was looking for—or the idea of it, anyway—in the one man she couldn't catch feelings for.

Which meant…she had to put them aside if her goal was still to convince Ian to take care of Henry—and that had to be her focus, as it had been from the start. She could give up her desires for her son; she'd been doing that since she'd discovered his unique needs and hadn't had a single regret yet.

Ian couldn't come first—she wouldn't let that happen.

Now, how to help him see that he was the best fit for Henry, if he couldn't be for her.

That was the real challenge. One she hoped she was up for.

CHAPTER FIVE

IAN'S LEG DIDN'T ache like it had the past few days. Jogging up and back to his truck to rescue the downed mountain biker had done a number on the muscle tissue around the sutures, but Casey's work held up.

He stretched it and found that the elasticity of Casey's stitches meant he could squat down to tie his shoes and even work a normal shift, which he'd done the past three days.

His and Casey's patient had been life-flighted to the clinic, where they'd been met by Jeff's wife and oldest daughter. Jeff had survived the first night, which is when the team of physicians at the Hoodsport clinic were most worried. He was transported two days later by ambulance to Seattle Memorial to address the rest of his injuries.

Now, the biggest hurdle Jeff faced was his leg. He'd had two compound fractures, which meant multiple surgeries to correct the alignment and remove bone fragments.

The first was that afternoon and Ian was driving to Seattle for the procedure. Since the clinic was technically a sister off-site property attached to the hospital, all the Hoodsport docs had privileges there as well.

Ian walked into the clinic more excited than normal. He loved his work, got deep meaning out of helping others right their lives and get back to what they loved to do. But this excitement was different. He could lie to himself and pretend he was just ready to see what the day brought them since the unseasonably sunny, fogless weather meant more foot traffic in the park.

But that would be a load of bull.

He wanted to see Casey.

One thing he wasn't going to do was inspect that feeling too closely, lest it lead to more…feelings. But he'd ride it out and let the excitement filter into his impending surgery. Starting with seeing if he maybe—just maybe—could have some company.

Ian shot off a text to the chief of the orthopedic department.

Hey, Rich. Not sure how staffing for today's femur and tibia repair is looking, but can I bring along our new NP to observe?

Professional, to the point, not at all indicative of the fact that Ian had dreamed about Casey the past few nights after working alongside her on Jeff's case.

The three dots in reply were immediate.

You bet. We're working bare bones today, so if they want to assist, they're welcome. As long as they did their onboarding already.

Ian couldn't keep the smile from his face as he replied.

Thanks. Done and done.

Again, the response was instant.

See you soon. If you two want to stay the night, the wife and I aren't using the condo. Feel free to relax and make a night of it. There are two bedrooms, by the way, haha. Didn't mean to imply anything… Anyway, drive safe.

Ian thought about that. About staying in Seattle, about showing Casey his favorite Thai food truck, maybe going to Pike's Place Market. Then his thoughts took a turn, and he wondered about not needing a second bedroom.

Knock it off, dude.

He'd had his fair share of intimate experiences with women willing to forgo the traditional dating scene that he wanted no part of. If he wanted that, he could have it—not that he was lacking humility, but he knew he was handsome by conventional standards and successful at that. Finding women to sleep with wasn't an issue.

But he didn't see Casey that way. He actually wanted to get to know her more, which was part of the "feelings" he didn't want to dive into too closely. Before asking her to join him on the trip to Seattle Memorial, he ran through the reasons Casey needed to remain a colleague and friend.

She's your colleague, like you already said. If you eff this up, you have to work alongside her, and the guys'll kill you for making it awkward.

Fine. Good point.

She's got a kid. Not just any kid, either. Henry had osteogenesis imperfecta, type IB. That meant he was at risk for all kinds of problems as he grew up, from broken bones to complex fractures. He was cool as hell, but…a complication when it came to Casey.

Partly because Ian couldn't help thinking about treatment plans with the boy and that wasn't his job. Even if he still took cases like that, he worked with Henry's mom, which made it a conflict of interest.

That's the part he couldn't share with her, not without hurting her. And he found that the last thing he wanted to do was be responsible for the look on Casey's face that she'd had when they'd talked about Ian's departure from Chicago just before Henry's appointment.

It was hurt, pure and simple.

And that's exactly what he'd do if he told her

that her desperate move to the Pacific Northwest to work with him at the clinic was the one thing that guaranteed he'd never be able to treat Henry, even if he had a change of heart with taking on complex cases like his. Well, the second. That he was feeling…something else for her? That was a nonstarter for so many reasons, but it also complicated things with Henry.

Speaking of the boy, his was the first face Ian saw when he got to his office in the new Hector Ruiz Clinic. He'd wanted something small, just a desk and place to consult with patients he would see from the local area, or who needed follow-up care. Nothing more. Greg had opted for—and self-funded—something more lavish, but that wasn't Ian's taste.

He'd brought in his teakwood desk from Hawaii and some photos of his adventures, a couch for clients, and a small fridge for drinks and food when he stayed late writing up charts.

Henry was stretched out on his couch, a comic book held over his head with one hand. The other petted a snoozing Scout, who didn't even flinch at his entrance. Ian tilted his head to see what Henry was reading. Superman, an old-school double edition.

Huh. Where'd he get something that cool?

It was such a cute scene, Ian hated to announce his arrival. But he was also curious about why the boy was in his office. And where his mother might be.

When Ian cleared his throat, Henry startled and the book fell on his face. He made a sharp cry and Ian rushed over to him. Scout jumped up from his spot on the floor and licked Henry's hand.

Sure enough, when Ian took the book off, Henry's nose was bleeding. His eyes were wide, as if he imagined he was in trouble.

"Hey, there, champ. I'm sorry I scared you. You okay?" He ran his thumbs lightly down the boy's nose. No break, thank goodness. Just must've hit a vessel with the corner of the thicker book.

"I'm fine," Henry said, sitting up and tilting his head forward like Ian would have suggested. He took the tissue Ian offered and made it into a second plug to staunch the bleed. This wasn't the boy's first rodeo. He was impressed. For five years old, the kid had a sense of how to take care of himself. "Sowwy 'bout the cowsh."

The plugged nose made it hard to understand Henry, but Ian got the gist.

"No worries, bud. Whatcha reading there?"

Henry's smile peeked from behind the tissue as Ian took the plug. "Superman. He's my favorite."

"Oh yeah?" Ian tossed the bloody tissue and made a new plug just in case. Scout watched the whole thing with interest. The dog was technically Greg's, but even though Greg had returned from Seattle three days ago, Scout had spent the past few nights with Ian at his house and curled up in his office each day. "Why's that?"

"He isn't scared of anything and nothing can hurt him. Isn't that cool?"

Ian's heart swelled three sizes. This poor kid. He'd never know a life without that kind of fear. Without worrying that everything he did might maim or kill him.

He cleared his throat, which was suddenly thick. "It's real cool. But don't forget, even Superman can be hurt by kryptonite. Everyone has something that can hurt them. A weakness that can be exploited."

"Explo—" Henry said.

"Sorry. Something that can be used against him by a bad guy."

Henry's eyes widened more, if that was possible. He was such a cute kid. "Huh. I didn't think about that. What's yours?"

Ian let that question sink in. He had a dozen right off the top of his head.

His own fear about losing people he loved.

Hurting himself and leaving Greg without a sibling.

Being so afraid of his past mistakes that he never fully relaxed into medicine again.

"I think the people I care about are mine," he finally settled on.

Henry nodded, and for a second, Ian considered

the fact that this kid had already earned a place amongst those he cared for. His mother had, too.

"Mine is my bones, obviously," he said, drawing out the last word as if he was a teenager and not a kid in kindergarten. He hugged Scout tightly and the dog let him. "But maybe Scout, too. My mom's is people, too. I think me, mostly."

Ian was speechless. The kid had an amazing ability to pick up on what was happening around him. When he had to track everything to make sure it couldn't cause him harm, hyperawareness was probably a side effect.

"Yeah, you're right. Where is she, by the way?"

A knock on the door stole Henry's attention. As if talking about her had the power to summon her, she called out.

"Henry?" the voice on the other side whispered. Ian stifled a smile. She must not know he was in there, either. Good on the kid for finding a place where he felt comfortable. Ian was a little honored it was in his space. "Henry, where are you?"

"Come on in, Casey," Ian said. She did, and upon seeing her son's blood-stained face, with a plug in one nostril, the color left her face, and she ran over to assess the damage. Ian could see the truth in Henry's statement. Casey's greatest weakness was her love for her son, no question. It was also her greatest joy. He'd never seen happiness on someone's face like he had when Casey talked about

Henry or joked with him. "He's fine. Just dropped the book."

She frowned, but her eyes held so much love in them as she cupped Henry's cheek.

"Henry, you have to be more careful," she admonished.

Henry shrugged away from her touch. "He said I'm fine, Mom."

She glanced at Ian, who nodded his agreement.

"Okay, well, I still want you to take care here. There's a lot you can hurt yourself on."

Henry's eye roll was epic. Ian stifled a smile. He'd be a handful in a couple years.

"*M-o-o-o-m*," he whispered. "You're embarrassing me." Henry nodded to Ian, whose skin warmed watching the two. It seemed to be a private moment, so he averted his gaze and made himself busy with what he'd gone in there for—the tablet so he could chart his progress with Jeff's ortho case.

"Sorry," she whispered back. Then, she glanced around and seemed to realize why she'd come there in the first place. In a normal tone, she asked, "Wait, why are you in here?"

Henry shrugged. "Scout was here and I like the couch. Plus, he has sodas."

Ian couldn't hold back the smile this time. "He's fine to use the space as long as we don't have a patient in here. And the sodas are all yours, buddy, but only if your mom says yes."

Casey shot him a tight smile. "Fine, but only if

you ask Dr. Matthews first next time. And only one soda a day."

"Fine. And I tried, but he wasn't here."

Ian held up his hand, inserting himself and unsure if it was appropriate to do so. "I mean it, he can hang in here with Scout any time he wants. He's a neat kid and I like having him around."

He meant it, too.

Henry had been around the past few days for the first half hour of Casey's shifts due to a scheduling conflict with Casey's mom's work. She'd been apologetic, but everyone loved chatting with the whip-smart kid about octopuses, hiking and his latest special interest—drawing people in the office. Plus, there was no one Scout loved more, aside from Ian. Greg didn't seem to mind, especially hearing how his dog had saved the mountain biker.

"Well, thank you. Anyway, I came to find you because grandma is in the lobby. She's going to take you to the library, then to Satchmos."

"Agaaain?" Henry complained. "We go to the library every day. Can't we do something cool like laser tag? Tommy went to laser tag and said it was *awesome*."

Ian winced as he watched Casey try to keep a smile for her son's sake. The reality was, so many of those activities would have to be monitored in order for Henry to participate, and would he resent that?

"Sometime. Just not with grandma. We'll find time for that and the aquarium soon."

Henry sighed, but then got up and hugged Ian, who squeezed him back gently. Even the wrong pressure from an embrace could hurt the kid and that was the last thing he wanted to do.

"See ya, Ian."

"See ya, kid. Thanks for hanging with Scout. And hey," he added. Henry turned around. At that moment, he looked like any other kid, hope and wonder blossomed in his smile. "You did good today, taking care of yourself and being brave like Superman. Not all heroes are strong like him—remember that."

Henry beamed and nodded.

Once Casey dropped him off, she came back, her lips in a grimace. "Sorry about that. He's getting to be so strong-willed I'm not sure how to rein him in most days."

"He's a good kid. I like him a lot." Ian glanced down at his paperwork, suddenly nervous. He liked more than Henry. He liked his mom, too. As a friend, of course. So why the nerves?

"He likes you, too. That's not the case with a lot of adults. They either treat him like nothing is wrong with him or everything is wrong. You treat him like a kid. I think that means a lot to him."

"I know what that's like, for people to pity you and treat you differently than you feel inside." She gazed up at him, questions in her eyes. He didn't know why he'd let that slip. It was true, of course—eight-year-old Ian had been the subject of pity, which hadn't matched the crippling guilt he'd felt at his and his sister's last interaction. He'd carried that with him for years until he was old enough to realize he'd just been a kid who'd had a normal kid squabble with a sibling. That had allowed a different sort of grief to come in, but he still understood the pity. However, he wasn't ready to open that door to Casey. Not to her, or anyone else. Hell, even he and Greg hadn't ever talked about it. Because what if they did and everything was different on the other side?

Maybe it's time to find out.

Maybe. But that was a risk he hadn't prepped for.

"Anyway, how long is Henry with your mom?"

"Till tomorrow night. They get one night a week together, more if my work schedule demands it, mainly to give me a break. I know that sounds cruel, but—"

Ian shook his head, cutting her off. "It doesn't sound bad at all. You and I talked about that when we first met." That seemed like eons ago, but it'd been mere days. What would months feel like as he got to know this woman and her son? "You can't parent him if you're not at your best and strongest."

"Thanks. I agree, just the mom guilt creeps in from time to time, you know?"

Ian nodded, even though, no, he didn't know. He lived alone, ate alone and even hiked and adventured alone. What did he know about meeting anyone's needs but his own?

For the first time in his life, he wondered if he'd been going about it all wrong. Life, that is.

He didn't have anyone to hold him accountable or keep him from doing what he loved, but at the same time, he noticed the flip side. He didn't have anyone to curl up with at night, either. After his and Greg's sister had died, he'd seen the grief etched on his parents' faces, in every movement they made. They'd died that day, too, leaving two young boys to all but raise themselves.

No wonder they'd both become doctors so no other families would have to suffer like Ian and Greg's had.

Except, under Ian's scalpel, one family had. They'd traveled to see Ian, specifically, and they'd lost everything. For years he'd wondered: If they'd gone anywhere else, would the outcome have been the same? The cause of the child's death was ruled an aortic aneurysm, which hadn't been detected on any of the scans—not even post mortem. But Ian couldn't get the nagging feeling out of his head that he'd missed something.

The family had sought him out to improve their son's quality of life, but quality of life meant nothing if there wasn't a life left at all. Which is why he couldn't consider taking Henry's case. If anything ever happened to that kid, not to mention on his watch…

He shook his head. Those were ghosts that had no business showing their faces here. He'd buried them, and they should stay that way. What had brought them to the surface, anyhow?

Oh, yeah. He'd allowed himself to wonder if those ghosts were too heavily influencing his life now. If he should chart a new course, allow. . .something else in.

Not with her, though. Even if he wasn't taking Henry's medical case, she was a colleague. On top of that, he had the pervasive thought that, even if they agreed on one night together, it might not be enough.

Oof. Plenty of reasons to steer clear.

Maybe that's why he couldn't believe his own ears when he blurted out, "Do you want to go to Seattle with me? We'll work on Jeff's case, then grab some dinner and maybe go out for a drink if you're up for it?"

What the hell? Having her assist on a surgery was one thing—making a date of it was a complete other. That was the last thing he needed.

Yeah, but you clearly want *it.*

Who cared what he wanted when that had the power to unravel the new life he was building for himself?

"Can I think about it?" she asked. He nodded, taking the hedging on her part as a lucky break on his. "I just got a young woman in with abdominal cramps. Might be pregnant based on her last menstrual cycle, and at eighteen, isn't sure that's a good thing or not."

"Of course. I'll be here till about eleven. I can let the ortho chief know we need his condo at any point since we don't need keys. It's a door code."

Like that detail mattered when he was kinda hoping she wouldn't agree to come at all, let alone stay the night. *Shut up, Matthews. Let her go to work and stop being weird.*

He was breathless as he realized if she said yes, he had to think about the best place for dinner and make sure it was good, but not romantic.

Oh, great. He'd really stepped in it now.

In hindsight, he'd been considering all morning asking her to assist in Jeff's surgery.

He craved seeing more of what she could do, what her style of practicing medicine was. And he'd also enjoyed the talks they had while they worked. Music, travel, books…they'd only skimmed the surface, but he got the sense they actually shared a lot in common and he wanted to find out just how much.

That's dangerous if you're not willing to let her in.

That wasn't true, the not-willing-to-let-her-in part. That's why his ghosts had made an appearance in the first place. Because meeting Casey had opened his eyes to what friendship outside his brother and Ethan might look like. It wasn't like he had to dive headfirst into a BFF situation or anything.

He'd just take the friendship slow and see where it went—up to a point. He'd put the brakes on things if they steered too close to those "feelings" he'd been having at certain times around her. At least, that's what he told himself. His heart argued that wasn't likely, but it had to be, right?

He realized with a sinking feeling he'd be bummed if she said no, which left him in gray territory.

Damn. Things were getting entirely too complicated. He thought she was attractive, liked watching her work and admired her role in Henry's life. That could equal a friendship, couldn't it?

An hour later and he'd gotten almost no work done, wondering if she'd come with him. He was like a damned teenager waiting for his crush to call back. Finally, at ten to eleven, the door pushed open and Casey poked her head in.

"We'd be spending the night?" she asked. He nodded, holding his breath. That wasn't a necessity, but he didn't want to risk what she was about to say. "And there are two bedrooms?"

He nodded again. "Yep." It's the only word he trusted himself with.

She smiled broadly and his heart pounded out a beat that sounded a little too much like a response to a *real* crush.

"Can we run by my house so I can grab my stuff for tonight?"

"Of course." He was shocked he got two words

out that time. Wow. He was a real Shakespeare, wasn't he?

"Okay," she said. "I'm in. Lemme grab my coat, and I'll meet you in the lobby."

He nodded, nerves fluttering in his chest like they did before a big climb. Great. So much for taking this slow. He was on a downhill ski slope and just had to hope there weren't any trees or cliffs he couldn't see or he might not recover from this fall.

CHAPTER SIX

THE DRIVE TO Seattle was everything Casey hoped it would be. Traveling with Ian was easy, almost too easy. She had to keep reminding herself this wasn't a date.

It was too easy to assume different intent when her whole life of late had been responsibility and service, devoid of anything resembling fun. Being kid-free allowed her to let her hair down, literally and figuratively. Throw in a good-looking, intelligent, single man, and her imagination went into overdrive.

Except…in the back of her mind were two flags reminding her that those feelings were taking her to rough seas if she followed them. For starters, Ian was a daredevil like Lawrence. Sure, she'd been adventurous at one point in her life, too, but she'd always known she wanted a family. Ian and Lawrence, however, seemed to share the notion that a family got in the way of adventure. And to her? Family was *everything.*

Second was her mission. She was holding out

hope that Ian would get to know Henry and agree to perform the surgery needed to give her son a better quality of life. If she fell for him, and it got in the way of what was best for Henry? She'd never forgive herself.

So why'd you say yes to coming at all? A valid question from the responsible part of her brain.

The complete answer to why she'd said yes was somehow grounded in a combination of what she needed to forget—that she was wildly attracted to the man and under different circumstances would like to see where the evening went with him—and what she desperately needed to remember. That he was off-limits, so this evening was just a work trip with some added fun at the end.

So she settled in, content just to enjoy her new colleague's company.

"You said you lived in Tucson, right? That's pretty landlocked."

"It was. But we'd drive to the northern part of the Sea of Cortez just over the Mexican border and dive, kayak, hike the foothills of the mountains, fish—anything we could to appreciate the weather and water."

"Do you…do you still do any of that?"

She shook her head. "No." She held in a sigh. Her life was good—content if not happy. She didn't want for anything and had no right to complain about what might have been. She'd lived a life of adventure and now had a small family she loved very much. Most people would never be as lucky as she'd been. "I don't, but it's okay. I like my life. And moving up here will be a whole new adventure."

"It will." Casey peered out the window as he slowed. They waited for two deer to cross the road but she felt him watching her. She turned and sure enough, his gaze was pinned to hers instead of the adorable wildlife. "I had no idea you had that kind of a past."

She laughed. "Because I'm so boring now?" The shock in his eyes made her laugh harder.

"No," he said, moving down the road now that the doe and fawn were out of harm's way. "That's not what I meant. It's just hard to imagine the woman I met that night—the loving mother and nurse practitioner with the beautiful, immaculate home and adorable son—with someone diving off the back of a boat. That's all."

She raised a brow. "Were you always this adventurous, then?"

He shook his head and gave a small chuckle. "Touché. You're right. No, I wasn't. I guess I've grown into this version of myself over time like you have." She nodded. "Do you miss it?"

"Every day," she answered honestly. Maybe when Henry was older, she could take day trips around Puget Sound and get back to that part of her she'd left behind when she'd become a mother. It was hard to imagine what that would look like with Henry, though. Would he be resentful that she could do all of that and more and he couldn't?

That was the conundrum—a mother was supposed to want more for her children than she ever had herself. She did want that for Henry, but the reality of what he could do was hindered by his physical limitations.

She rolled down the window when they got off the highway and let the warm spring air into the cab. "Is this okay?" she asked. He nodded and put his own down as well. Her hair swirled around her and she closed her eyes. With the unseasonably warm weather and a hint of salt from the Salish Sea in the air, she could almost pretend she was back in Mexico with her parents before her world had gone off track.

She'd never trade Henry for anything, but there were days she wondered why she had to endure losing a husband in order to have the best thing in her life. It wasn't just her husband's death that had taken him from her, either. It was their change in lifestyle that he hadn't wanted to endure. So he'd stayed stagnant and she'd pivoted.

When he'd died, they were already so estranged—had been since Henry's birth. It felt like a lifetime ago and it'd only been five years. What would the next five years hold for her? If days like today were any indication of where her life was headed, she wouldn't complain.

She and Ian spent the last fifteen minutes of the

drive in silence, but it wasn't uncomfortable. If anything, it felt—to her, at least—as if they'd known one another for years.

What does that mean to you? her heart whispered. She didn't know. Because with the comfort came worry in the same shape as it had been since she'd had Henry—the angular corners dividing what she might want, might desire for herself in her most selfish moments, and what was best for her son.

What she desired? To explore the pulsing energy between her and Ian. To see where it might lead, even just for a night. *Couldn't you give yourself that one pleasure*? her heart wanted to know. *For all the other sacrifices you've made?*

No. Her brain answered with finality. Not this man. Literally anyone else. Not Ian, though.

Henry is all that matters, she repeated. *Don't let this get in the way.*

Her focus was firmly in place as they pulled up to the hospital and were met by the head of ortho, a physician named Richard Coker. Casey had heard good things about the man; his reputation was almost as stellar as Ian's had been before he stopped working in Chicago.

"Welcome to Seattle Memorial, Ms. Larsen. We're excited to have you," he said.

She glanced up at the building in front of them and was filled with awe. The hospital she'd worked at in Tucson was a lot like the tan interior of her home—safe, sterile and yet largely without personality.

Seattle Memorial was a dark wood and glass work of art. Her mouth fell open.

"It's beautiful, isn't it?"

"It's spectacular. I'm lucky to be here. Thanks for the invitation."

"It's a standing contract that you share privileges here, and from your reputation, we're the lucky ones. But the invitation today comes from this guy," he said, slapping Ian on the back. Ian's face got red immediately.

Casey shot Ian a look. *He* was the one who had asked for her to come? Not the chief of ortho? Ian hadn't expressly said the hospital wanted a team, but she'd made that assumption. Then again, he *had* added on dinner and a hockey game. He shrugged and his piercing gaze was unreadable. When Rich gestured them in, Ian broke her gaze and followed him through the tall wooden doors for staff.

Nerves flitted over her skin, making her clammy.

Oh my gosh. Does he think this a date?

Her own resolve to think of it as anything but wavered.

She pasted on a smile and joined the men inside. The rest of the building was as magnificent as the outside's curb appeal. It had a gym for staff and family visiting long-term patients, state-of-the-art surgical suites for every specialty of medicine, a neonatal unit that had won awards for its efficiency and comfort, and a cafeteria that boasted a menu rivaling some of the nicer restaurants she'd been to in Tucson.

She'd be jealous of the doctors and nurses who got to work here every day if she wasn't madly in love with her own new clinic. The past few days there, in a gorgeous, small but still modern and state-of-the-art facility, surrounded by water, forest and mountains, she felt *home* for the first time in her life.

The orthopedic wing was just as nice as the rest of the hospital, and the good news was, she could help out there whenever she wanted and they needed her assistance. Maybe, down the road when Henry and her mom could join her, they could all do a weekend in the city. She could pick up a shift and he could go to the aquarium.

Until then, she'd enjoy these perks and take solace in the fact that her world had just expanded tenfold in so many ways.

Workwise, anyway.

"This was a helluva save," Rich said, showing them to the staff locker room where they could change and store their belongings. "Greg said a dog found the mountain biker?"

"Our family dog, Scout, yeah. Might turn out to be on our payroll if he keeps that up," Ian said.

Casey's stomach clenched at his casual mention of the word "family."

Rich laughed. "Well, lemme know if you need

anything. I'll be out of touch for an hour or so with the new interns, but after that I'll be available by pager."

"Thanks again," Ian said. Casey echoed it.

"Of course. Oh, and you got the code for the condo, right?"

Ian nodded and accepted scrubs on their behalf from a nurse.

"Yep. Thanks for that, too. It'll be nice not to rush back in the dark after this surgery."

Casey swallowed hard. *See? The "date" you're worried about is just pragmatic.* His nonchalance about the whole spending the night in town together thing helped calm her down. She needed to get a grip if she expected to keep a professional relationship with the guy.

She relaxed and a real smile formed. This was going to be a cool surgery.

Rich nodded and took off down a long hallway lined with photographs of the Olympic Mountains and Puget Sound. At the end was a framed photo of an octopus. She'd have to remember to take Henry to see it.

"Okay," Ian said. "Let's do this."

They changed and met outside Jeff's room. He was already prepped and intubated, and once again, Casey was impressed by the efficiency with which the hospital operated.

Ian went over the plan with her. He was going to work on the femur first, since that would take the most amount of time and hardware. Then, they'd move on to the tibia, where they'd have more of a sense of what they'd need.

"I'll have you be my right hand in there if you're comfortable with it."

He'd said as much in the truck on the drive over, but with the scans in front of them, it was easier to see what he'd need. She nodded.

"That's great, but can I ask a question?"

"Always. That's part of why you're here—so we can get to know how one another works. It'll help us speak the same language when we're working together at the clinic."

See? Practical. Professional. Not *a date.*

"Is there a reason you won't fix the dorsal bone first so it isn't..." She searched for the best word to use, but they were running out of time. "So it isn't flopping around while you place the intramedullary rod? His tibia was broken in two places, and I worry it'll get in the way."

Flopping wasn't exactly a professional word, but he got the sense of what she meant. She'd never felt confident sharing her ideas for cases with her attending physicians before, partly because she didn't have the degree they had. But something about Ian made her feel as if she could do that safely.

Ian stopped where he was and gazed down at her. He pulled up the chart and nodded. He rubbed his chin, as if he was contemplating her advice. Doubt filled her. He was a world-renowned orthopedic surgeon. Why was she telling him what to do?

"Sorry," she said. "I didn't mean to second-guess your approach. I'll just—"

"No," he said, shaking his head and putting a hand on her shoulder. Heat pulsed beneath his palm, warming the skin beneath her scrubs. "That's a good idea."

"Oh," she whispered. "Okay."

"Let's do that, and—Casey?" She gazed up at him.

"Yes?"

"Never feel like you have to keep your thoughts to yourself. I want to hear all your ideas. I know I speak for Greg, Erin and Reese, too," he added.

"Sounds good. And in case I forget to tell you later, thanks for inviting me," she said. "This is a cool opportunity."

He nodded, and there was that flash of color on his cheeks again. What was that about? Paired with his intense gaze from earlier, there had to be more to the story. Unfortunately, he wasn't saying anything, nor was his thin smile readable.

"Yep. Glad to have you" was all he said. Great. She was reading into everything.

Calm down, Casey. You can be around a cute guy and not lose your mind.

Could she, though? All evidence pointed to the contrary.

They masked and gloved up and went through

the sliding door. The anesthesiologist gave the go-ahead.

They began with the two fractures in the tibia, using an internal fixation due to the more serious injury to the femur above. The risk of infection was too great to place the hardware on the outside of the skin.

"Just so you know, I don't have a set plan for complicated orthopedic surgeries like this. I'm really glad you spoke up. This is a better approach now that we're here."

She smiled below her mask. It felt good to be validated, especially by a doctor like Ian, with the reputation for executing brilliant surgeries over the course of his first career in Chicago.

"Why don't you? Have a plan, I mean."

He shrugged and held out his hand. "I need the next set of screws," he told the nurse, who handed them over. To Casey, he said, "I learned over time that every case is different. Even if two patients have the same spiral fracture, their comorbidities are different, their health and lifestyle come into play and even their age will factor in."

"That makes sense. In Tucson, I assisted on a lot of hip replacements, but there was always protocol for that."

Ian nodded. "Yep. That checks out. A lot of docs want the continuity of procedure because they claim there's less room for error, but I always found the opposite. Doing everything the same for people who are built differently is asinine. At least to me."

"Hmm. I never thought about that," she said. Part of that was her own fault—not asking questions, keeping the status quo at work so she didn't make waves and lose the stellar health insurance that cared for Henry. All that was different now. The clinic, and the docs there, made it clear they welcomed her mind and questions. She'd grow as a practitioner if she wanted to.

And she did. The adrenaline she'd felt caring for Jeff the first time came back. It was as if pieces of her were coming alive again after being dormant for years. They itched to move, to flex, to dance like a sleeping limb after waking up.

They worked in silence for a few minutes, but she was full of questions that surfaced thanks to his comments. It was a long procedure, but wasn't nearly as complicated or time-consuming as the femur would be. They had time to talk, right?

She'd never been in a long surgery with anyone she wanted to know more about. Until now, that was. Her first inclination was to ask him what had happened in Chicago to make him leave his practice—especially because of its implications for Henry's future. But now, surrounded by nurses and the anesthesiologist, wasn't the time. Maybe over dinner. Instead, she opted for something she hoped was more generalized in getting to know him—

without seeming like she wanted anything more than friendship.

It would be tough walking this line with him.

"Are you okay if I ask you a question? Or do you prefer to work in quiet?"

She loved the way his eyes crinkled, like he was smiling behind the mask.

Keep it professional, her head warned.

"Tell me about your family since you've met mine." There. That was just her asking about the man she'd be working with. No big deal.

"Um," he said, his eyes losing the smile. Oh no, what had she done? "You've met mine as well. It's just Greg and I now." Her heart lurched and she forced herself to focus on the patient.

"I'm so sorry. We don't need to talk about this now, here..." She glanced at the nurses, but they were on the other side of the room, prepping a tray and the anesthesiologist was monitoring their patient.

He shook his head. "No, it's okay. It's a part of my fabric and talking about it probably helps. It's really simple, actually. We lost our sister to a negligent doctor and his treatment of what should have been a routine appendectomy. The medical malpractice lawsuit my parents sued the hospital for is what funded both our medical schools. It's also what all but killed them both. The money we got was supposed to replace the love that shriveled up when we lost her, but as anyone who's been through something similar can attest, there isn't enough money in the world."

Casey blinked back the heat that built behind her eyes. How horrible to bury one of your children. It was her worst nightmare and constant worry. Unfortunately, there was a strong risk she would be faced with that possibility one day.

"You and Greg…" she said. Her voice was foreign to her, a shadow of a whisper. Their pain was palpable. How were the strongest men she'd ever met also people who had endured losing a sibling they loved so much? It hurt her to hear, and she'd barely known them longer than a week.

"There isn't a day I wake up that I wish I wasn't paying off student loans instead of having something to tell my sister and knowing she'll never hear it. That I don't think about how she'll never see the men we became, the doctors we're becoming. She'd love the clinic—she was by far the most adventurous of us."

"I'm so sorry," Casey said. The room was quiet, only the beep of the heart rate monitor to break the oppressive silence. "There's nothing worse."

"Maybe." He met her gaze over their masks, and she was surprised to see that his eyes were even more intense when the rest of his face was covered and not drawing focus.

Was he referring to why he'd left his Chicago practice? Oh, gosh. What could be worse than losing someone you loved? She didn't dare ask, but she would tonight. Not because of what it meant for Henry, but because she found she cared. She wanted to help if she could.

He moved from closing the tibia to the femur repair while she rolled her shoulders back and stretched them.

"Do you need a break?"

She shook her head. "I'm okay. I'm here till the end."

It shocked her to realize that she meant more than just the surgery. She would be here while he told his story, and while she wrote hers moving forward. As friends, as colleagues… She let the rest drift off—no end to that sentence, but no room for it, either.

"Okay. I'm going to place the intramedullary rod into one side, pull the femur over it, and use valium to relax the muscle. The internal fixation device for the fibula should hold up to that. Can I answer your question while we work? This is gonna be a long one."

She nodded. "Let's do this."

He called for a scalpel and opened up Jeff's thigh. Just as Ian opened his mouth to continue, he was cut off by a shrill alarm that filled the room and hurt Casey's ears.

Somehow, Ian's voice rang over it as the anesthesiologist adjusted the dials on the medications.

"He's coding."

"What happened?" Casey asked. Her pulse was

going wild, as were her fears. They couldn't get this far and lose him—they couldn't.

"His body isn't handling the anesthesia for this long," the anesthesiologist said.

For the first time since she'd moved, Casey longed for the easy patients she'd had in Tucson. At least there, no one's life had been on the line.

At the same time, she was ashamed to admit it—and wouldn't if she was asked—but she also felt more alive than ever by trying to bring back a patient this close to death.

Ian's eyes were lined with the same fear coursing through her bloodstream, and she vowed then to do whatever she needed to do to help him get past whatever ghosts haunted him.

But first, they needed to save Jeff's life for a second time.

CHAPTER SEVEN

"HE'S LOST SINUS," he called out. The nurses and Casey leaped into action, each stationing themselves around Jeff's body, ready to do what Ian needed them to do.

Right now, that was just chest compressions, and he took that on himself.

Ian pressed the heels of his palms over Jeff's heart and leveraged his weight. He focused on their patient, but over his mask, he watched Casey's eyes widen. He'd be willing to bet she'd never lost a patient on the table. Not from what she'd said about her previous hospital.

Jeff's rhythm didn't come back, and the beeping increased, alerting them to other failures. This had been a long surgery, and his body was under a lot of stress.

"Come on," he said through gritted teeth, pressing harder on his patient's chest. "Please don't do this to her. To me."

To your own family.

The trauma of what he'd been through—what

his patient's family had been through in Chicago—hung in the air like a spirit haunting him. How quickly it all came rushing back in the height of a new, unrelated event.

There had been risk all along and everyone had been aware of it, but in the end, it wasn't those risks that had killed his young patient. It was the unrelated risks inherent to every surgery, every procedure…the unknown.

Still, he'd felt *guilty.* Like his need to fix what was fine and good enough had led to the worst imaginable thing. If he'd never started doing the bone rodding for OI patients—an unnecessary but potentially life-enhancing surgery—would the boy have died when his aneurysm burst? Maybe not but they'd never know, would they?

The guilt resurfaced and his own pulse went erratic. Part of it was from sharing about his sister. He'd thought that was benign territory, but apparently nothing was. His breath wouldn't come past his throat.

Until a gloved hand set atop his. He glanced up between chest compressions and met Casey's gaze. It was a lighthouse in the dark, guiding him to a safe port. She didn't say anything, just gave a nod.

He nodded back and called for more relaxants for Jeff. The man's heart was going to explode if his body didn't calm down. The nurse nodded and increased the dose on his IV. Immediately, Jeff's sinus rhythm returned and the anesthesiologist exhaled.

"That was close," the other doc said. "I don't know why he decompensated like that—he looked okay on my end."

"Here, too," Casey added.

"Hmm," Ian said. "I'll keep an eye on his numbers while we finish up. But we need to be quick. Casey, are you okay going forward?"

"I am. I'm fine, just worried about our patient. Thanks for asking, though." She smiled and he could see it in her eyes above the mask.

Ian nodded and touched Casey's hand with the back of his.

"Thank you," he whispered to her. "I haven't been that close to losing a patient in a while. I'm sorry I froze."

"You're fine. Will you tell me why, though?"

He nodded. He owed her that much, at least. He pulled the rod the rest of the way through and began the repair while he talked.

"At dinner, if that's okay?"

She gave a short nod and he fastened the rod and devices needed to keep it in place.

They wrapped up the surgery in silence, the steady beeping of Jeff's monitors alerting them to how he was doing. He didn't have another incident and they closed without concern.

"He's got to get through the night, but I think we're in the clear," Ian said. Relief coursed through him as they tugged off their masks and gloves and went back to the locker room.

"I'm glad I came here," she said, her voice sounding a million miles away. "Not just to Hoodsport, but Seattle. With you."

"I'm glad you came, too. Even though poor Jeff probably doesn't want to see us ever again." Casey chuckled as they made their way out of the hospital and into Ian's truck for the drive to the condo. The tension from holding back what would have been his knee-jerk response—that he really liked everything they did together—dissipated with her laughter. "So what makes you glad you came to Hoodsport?"

There. Nice, easy territory, somewhere in the vague no-man's-land between friend and the *more* that had been on his mind, the *more* he couldn't follow through on no matter how much his libido wished he could. Hell, that his heart wished was possible.

"I love the green, the sense of play right outside the door. The peace of the forest and water and where they meet..." She drifted off and his skin tingled with awareness. "I can't wait to get settled, to make my actual home match what I feel inside since being here."

"Not beige?" he teased.

She laughed harder at that. "No. Not beige. That was how the house came and it matched the furniture I brought from Tucson. But it isn't…me anymore."

He took advantage of a stoplight to peer over at her and was in awe of her natural beauty, especially after a full day of surgery. Her skin was flushed and her eyes bright as she took in the skyline of Seattle. To be fair, he'd been here a dozen times the past year and didn't think he'd ever get sick of it. He wasn't a city guy—maybe hadn't ever been. If he hadn't been afforded the opportunity to perform the kind of surgeries he'd taken on in the first half of his career, he'd have moved someplace like Hoodsport much sooner.

As it was, he was glad he'd landed where he had. Seattle was nice to live near and was surrounded by just the kind of recreation that Ian loved.

He pulled up to the condo and parked in the garage allocated for the waterfront owners. He'd stayed there before after a long surgery—Rich kept the place for just that reason, and even rented it out from time to time to traveling nurses in the area.

"Wow," Casey said when they got out of the elevator. The whole living room that the elevator opened on to was a wall of windows that boasted a spectacular view of Puget Sound and the ferries coming into the city. It also gave them a peek at the Space Needle from the left set of windows. "This is *amazing*."

Rich had impeccable taste, Ian gave him that.

She gasped when he led her to the master suite.

It had a California King bed with a teakwood headboard and was outfitted with matching furniture. A desk and chair were in one corner, but there was still so much space.

"Wait till you see the bathroom." He led her through the doorless entryway and she laughed.

"This is unreal. I can't believe people live like this." Ian smiled. "I don't think I'd ever leave if I lived here. Look at that tub," she said, sitting on the edge to see the view from that window. It showed off Bainbridge Island and wasn't a place he'd complain about spending time at, either.

"You'd love my Chicago place, then. I was hardly there, but the river was my landscape and you could swim laps in my tub."

"You surgeons know how to live." She laughed, but he thought about that. Did he? Sure, he knew how to have nice things—simple but lovely expressions of his tastes and accumulated wealth.

But did he have the right priorities? With Casey next to him, a successful surgery where he'd played it safe and smart, he felt like maybe he was on the right track, finally. She sat on the bed and tucked her knees up under her.

"You can have this room. Unless you want to see the rest first?" he asked.

She yawned. "Maybe later? I'm ashamed to admit that if I don't eat soon, you won't like me much."

He smiled, wondering what it would actually

take for him to stop liking her. If there was a pill, he'd take it. Anything to stave off the want that coursed through him when he was in the same space as Casey and a mattress that spanned the length of her.

"Do you want to order food in, then? We did have a pretty long day in the surgery. You must be wiped."

She smiled and though he could see exhaustion in her shoulders, he also saw excitement in her eyes as she shook her head.

"No. I haven't been here before, not really. And I had Henry with me, so—"

"Say no more," he told her. A sudden, pervasive desire to show her the whole city, everything he loved about it, overwhelmed him. That wasn't possible, but dinner was. He knew just where to take her. "Let's get dressed and I've got just the place."

"I've only got jeans and a nice top. Will that be enough?"

He chuckled. "You'll find out soon enough that jeans and just about anything is the official uniform of the Pacific Northwest. Aside from a fancy Broadway production at Christmas, that'll get you in anywhere."

She clapped her hands and the excitement he'd seen in her face radiated through each of her limbs as if they hadn't just done a seven-hour surgery. "Do I have time to shower and change? The only thing I need more than food is to rinse the surgery off me."

"If your hunger won't stop you, we've got all the time you need." While Casey headed for her ensuite bathroom, he shut the bedroom door and headed to the living room, sank onto the generous couch and let his eyes drift closed for a moment.

The door opened. His eyes shot open and he thought he must be dreaming. Casey stepped out and his breath caught in his throat.

"Um," he managed. *Nice. Real smooth.* "Wow. You look great."

That was an understatement. She had on jeans and a top, just as she'd mentioned. But what she'd failed to articulate was that the top was a sheer floral number with what looked like a black bra underneath. He didn't want to look too closely, but he thought it might be black lace.

Her dark jeans were painted on, too. Topping the whole thing off were a pair of black booties with a wedge heel and understated gold jewelry—a fish necklace and pair of earrings—that complemented the top.

It was her makeup and hair that did him in, though. She'd let her hair go curly, and put just a hint of mascara and eye shadow on so that her already captivating eyes shone like framed jewels.

"Thanks," she said. "I rarely get a chance to wear heels or makeup, so I've got to admit it feels good to be…well, something else besides a nurse and mom."

"Well, it suits you. I'll be the luckiest man in Seattle tonight."

Her cheeks turned as pink as the peonies on the shoulder of her top.

Good grief. This woman is amazing.

It wasn't the first time he'd thought it, either. He'd been in awe of her as a medic, then as a mother, and now he got to see her as a woman. Not one bit of her disappointed.

Not exactly a recipe for ignoring her pull on him, either.

"Um," he said again. He was a real wordsmith tonight. "I'm gonna just be a sec, then we'll go eat."

He couldn't shower fast enough—not only because she was starving, but just so he could be back in her presence, period.

In less than a quarter of an hour, they were in a cab, knees touching in the small back seat. His stomach fluttered like he was taking her out on a date. And for the life of him, nothing he thought about—her position in the clinic, her son, her newness to town—none of it dissuaded him from that singular thought.

Because you like her. As more than a colleague or friend.

He did, sorta. He liked her as a friend too, though. But yeah, he was also as attracted as hell to her in a way that said "more than friends."

"Remind me to get on your friend's wifi when we're back so I can call my mom. My phone doesn't seem to want to connect to any of the cell towers."

"Hmm. Is it like that in Hoodsport?" he asked.

"Sometimes. I think it's just my phone revolting because we're in more moisture than it can handle. I wonder if I'll ever feel the same. Right now, I love the rain in all its forms."

He smiled. "I do, too. Greg said he might need to head south or dry—or both—in the winters, but the seasonal affective disorder hasn't gotten me yet.

"By the way," Ian said, "if you want to go take care of the phone tomorrow before we head home, I'm happy to take you."

"Thank you. Let's see how we do for time. I can always drag my mom and Henry into the city with the bribe of coming to the aquarium."

"Will that work on your mom?"

She laughed. "No. You're right. I'll have to promise her a spa treatment of some sort. Is Seattle too hippie for that?"

He shook his head. "Nope. Hotels and spas are as bougie as they come here."

Casey clapped. "Lovely. Now if I can find a way to take my mom there and sneak a massage for myself, I'll be golden."

He nibbled on the inside of his lip. "I can take Henry to the aquarium if you'd like," he told her. "You and your mom could take the afternoon and do something for yourselves. Goodness knows you both deserve it." If he could capture the expression on her face, he'd quit medicine and paint it on every canvas he could find.

"You'd do that? He's a lot to take on, though," she challenged. But the overall look in her eyes—pure hope—said she didn't mind the offer.

"I think I'm one of the safest bets to care for Henry, don't you think?" There was a pause, and he wondered what she must be thinking. That as a professional he was a safe bet. But how did his life look to her otherwise? "And don't worry," he added. "What I do on my own time is for me. I know Henry has other limitations and would make that my priority."

She smiled the widest grin he'd ever seen, and he knew he'd won that argument. "Yeah, I guess you are a safe bet. Thank you for the offer. I'd like to say no, that it wouldn't be necessary, or that it's too generous to accept, but I'd love it, to be honest. Does that make me a monster?'

He laughed and shook his head. "Absolutely not. It makes you a tired mother. And I wouldn't have offered if I didn't want you to take me up on it. We'll make a plan tonight at dinner."

"I'd like that," she whispered. He locked that away. The woman was in desperate need of feeling like something other than a person who satisfied everyone else's needs other than her own. If he could give that to her…

The need to be that person surprised him, mostly

because it implied that he wanted…more from her. And more wasn't anything he had to give at the moment. Damn. He'd better figure that out if he wanted to keep them both from getting hurt.

They pulled up to the restaurant and she smiled.

"I've heard of this place," she said. The constant awe in her voice, like each experience she had was amazing and inspiring, made him want to keep providing those moments for her. The thrill of her joy was as great as what he felt on the side of a peak or mountainside.

Hmm. Interesting development.

"It's my favorite in town, and I'm sorry to say that last week *The Seattle Times* did a rave piece about it, so it's about to become harder to get into than Fort Knox. But I know the chef—saved his son from losing his leg in a fall last year. We can come anytime we want."

The "we" hung in the thick sea air between them. He didn't reach to reclaim it, to draw it back in. He'd meant it.

"That's amazing."

He smiled and put his hand on the small of her back, guiding her into the small Italian restaurant. The maître d' recognized Ian and sat them at a small window table for two that looked out over Pike's Place Market, the world-renowned seafood marketplace.

They sat and perused the menu—or at least Casey did. Ian couldn't keep his eyes off her, at how she lit up with every new line she read. At one point, after he'd ordered them a bottle of wine, she bit her lip when the server asked if they wanted the bruschetta Ian normally ordered.

"Yes, please," she said. It was spoken with reverence, and man…he was addicted. The bruschetta arrived in less than a minute, meaning they'd already assumed Ian's order. He loved this place. She took a bite and grinned. "This is fantastic," she said.

A crumb rested on her lip, and he used his thumb to brush it off. The blush that followed made him want to phone in the rest of the evening and go back to the condo. Where his imagination led him next was so far off-limits, he might as well be in deep space.

Relax. Just enjoy her. Get to know her more—that's what today was supposed to be about, right?

It was. Too bad, his brain took that eight steps further than "What's your favorite color?" or "What would be your favorite dessert if you could only order that one for the rest of your life?"

As if she'd read his mind, she glanced up and, before he could ask anything on his list of curiosities about her, asked one of him.

"Can I ask you a personal question?"

Ian nodded as he poured a second glass of wine for them both. Too late to back down now.

"What happened in Chicago? Was it about your sister?" *Oof.* He'd expected this question at some point, but it still stole the breath from his chest like he'd been gut-punched.

"Sort of. I don't think I ever got over a fight I had with her right before she went to the hospital. I was only eight and she never came home." She gasped and never took her gaze from him. The way she listened made him feel safe, cared for. Saying these things wasn't as uncomfortable as he'd thought it might be. "I know that stayed with me when I became a doctor, but it didn't directly affect my decision to leave Chicago, no."

"What did? We don't have to talk about it, it's just… I don't know if you were aware, but it was the day before Henry and I were flying in for our appointment."

"I'm sorry," Ian said. It was almost a whisper.

"I know. We—we pivoted."

"How so?" He needed to know, needed to hear this.

She heaved a deep sigh and took a long sip of wine.

"Well, we flew into Chicago anyway and waited outside the ortho center in case you came back. On day two, the nurse came to the parking lot to let me know you'd cleaned your office out in the middle of the night and wouldn't be back." He took her hand. All the pain he'd caused by being so wrapped in his own grief. "I must've cried for an hour until Henry told me he was hungry. That's when we went to lunch next to the Chicago Aquarium, which led to him seeing his first Pacific octopus. It was worth that alone, but I'm just curious—what made you feel you had to leave medicine altogether."

The appetizer came and he motioned that she dive in, which she did.

"My patient was a kid a little older than Henry. He had type three osteogenesis imperfecta and his parents read about my previous studies. They reached out—much like you did—to ask if I would do bone rodding to give him quality of life…and perhaps a longer life, too."

"I've heard it's got good outcomes when it works. But it's risky," she said.

His skin felt warm, but he continued. "It is. It was. They were made aware of the risks, and I thought—"

"That it would be better than bisphosphonates?" Casey asked. She knew her stuff, but of course she did. She'd likely considered all the same treatments for Henry.

"Yes. More risk, more reward, is how I used to operate." In all areas of his life. But medicine was the one place he realized he couldn't afford to.

"He didn't make it?" she asked. Her voice was thick, like his.

He shook his head. "His young body was strong, even with his condition. But he suffered an aneurysm we didn't catch. I should have done more scans, looked for better options—"

Again, her hand brushed his. "I don't know what

the scans did or didn't say, but I'll bet you did all that. I researched you, you know. You were impeccable. That's a tragic accident, but it could happen to anyone, no matter the risk of the surgery." She paused. "And you gave them hope they would have chased to the next doctor. Any parent in that situation would want options."

His throat was warm and dry, thinking about Henry on that table. He'd only just gotten to know the boy, but he already cared for him deeply.

"Thanks. Anyway, now you know why I left, and why I can't treat Henry. I'm not too scared to operate, to make the tough calls, or I wouldn't be here at all. But it's too much to consider young lives like that and see the possibilities shrouded in risk and pain. Not when Henry can live a good, loving life without it."

She seemed to consider this as she slid a slice of bread through the sauce left from the appetizer. Her color had changed, as if the food had done quick work of improving her mood.

"Thanks for talking to me about what you went through," Casey said. "I can't imagine that the past few years have been easy for you."

Ian shook his head. "They haven't, but that's all changed recently," he said.

Her eyes did that thing again, where they filled with hope. He had to change the topic before he followed that hope back to the bedroom and made her forget she'd ever been less than appreciated.

"Can I ask one in return?"

"Of course," she said. "I asked you plenty."

"What happened to your husband?"

She let out a small sigh. "I knew the moment you asked that this is where things were leading. It's only fair, given what you shared. But I'll warn you—this wine will mean the story might be longer than you'd like."

"Take the time you need. I'm not going anywhere."

He leaned in. That was the thing. He'd asked because he was curious, because he wanted to know every small thing about her as well as the big things. What she ate on her toast, how she curled up with a book at night, what she wore to bed…

That last item might be elevated to "big things" status, so he added it to the list. The wine was making him brave, where she said it made her more willing to share. For the first time, he was actually curious—who knew where the night would end?

"Anyway, Lawrence and I met through diving and a shared sense of adventure. We fell in love pretty quickly and got married even faster." Ian tamped down a flash of envy for a man he'd never met. Especially because it wasn't like he wanted either love or marriage. But he did sorta want Casey. He forced himself to focus. "We had a lot of fun the first couple years, and then I got pregnant."

The way in which she said that—as if it was

something negative—didn't match the light in her eyes while she said it.

"He wasn't pleased?"

She shook her head. "It's not that. He was, sort of. Until I got the news that Henry's diagnosis would change the way he lived—and therefore how we lived while we helped take care of our son. Lawrence actually didn't find any of this out until I'd known a week, since he was on a rock climbing trip without me at the time of the scan. He 'wasn't checking his phone.' It was a pretty lonely time, actually."

Ian's jealousy became rage. He knew the rest of the story before she told it. Ian would bet his next paycheck that Lawrence kept his lifestyle while asking Casey to give up hers. And of course she would. Just look at the way she cared for her son.

With each word that confirmed his suspicions, Ian grew more incensed.

"I'm sorry. You deserve better. You both do."

"It doesn't matter now, does it? He died two years ago and lost the most amazing kid that's ever existed, all thanks to his ridiculous need to chase a high. Like any other addict, he needed a bigger fix each time, until it killed him. It's his loss that he didn't get to know Henry while he was alive, that he'll never get that chance again. What a waste."

Ian felt that in each of his cells. Was it his own biology that was failing him, pushing him toward his own addiction that might kill him someday, or was he shutting down the parts of him that were supposed to keep him safe?

"I hope you don't mind me saying all of that. It's a lot, I know."

It was. More than he would normally accept. But he still found himself saying, "Not a chance." It might damn him, but to make sure she didn't feel the way some jerk made her feel about her life and her choice to do the right thing by her child? It might be worth the fall.

When they both reached for the last piece of bread, their fingers brushed, and he was truly surprised there wasn't an actual flame where the heat blossomed on his skin.

Hell, he wanted her something fierce. But there was a Henry-sized boulder between them, and a thousand reasons she would run for the hills if he let her closer. He couldn't give in to the fire, even if all he wanted was for it to consume him.

"Henry's a good kid," he told her, putting his phone on silent and away. This was a topic that would pour water on the flames of his growing need for this woman—talking about her son. "I'm lucky to get to work with his mom and get to know him better."

Her face took on a pretty shade of pink that he attributed to embarrassment since the temperature in the dining room hadn't gone up at all. Okay, maybe he'd thought wrong about that. Dammit. Was anything safe to talk about with her? Even the silence was charged at this point.

"Thank you," she admitted. "That means more to me than you'll ever know." Her hand was on the table, between their seats, and before he could think too much about it, he grabbed it and squeezed. The heat from before turned into a blaze and the only thing that burned in its wake was his ability to stay away and make smart choices where Casey was concerned.

She squeezed back and gazed up at him with wide eyes. He saw more questions, but also something he recognized in his own eyes reflected back in hers.

Desire.

Whether it was for a kiss, an embrace, a night together or more…he didn't know or care. They could discuss it later. Right now, he just wanted to feel the newness of this, whatever it was or wasn't.

His heart pounded out a tattoo of longing he'd never experienced before. Is this what liking someone felt like? If so, maybe it wasn't all that bad.

The entrées arrived just as he twisted her hand so that it was wrapped in his, their fingers intertwined.

"Sorry," she said, pulling away. "I didn't mean to—"

He held her tighter.

"No apologies," he growled. "Want to get out of here?" She nodded, the corners of her mouth turned up in a gentle smile. To the server, he simply said, "We're gonna need these to go, please. And the check. As soon as possible."

CHAPTER EIGHT

CASEY DIDN'T THINK about her son, her mother, her new home that needed splashes of color and life… She didn't think about anything except Ian's hand in hers.

And the utter horror of knowing she'd shaved her legs that morning by some slim stroke of stupidity. What had her mother told her?

Don't shave on a first date, then you won't be tempted to... She didn't finish the thought since she definitely couldn't…*wouldn't*…be sleeping with Ian.

It was just nice to hold his hand. To give into that simple pleasure. Even if it did send her imagination careening off a cliff taller than Hurricane Ridge.

Because something had happened between the surgery and dinner. Something about the way he'd looked at her when she'd come out of the bathroom—like she was more than just a mom or nurse or colleague, or even a friend.

He'd gazed at her like she was a woman, and maybe even an attractive one at that. Had she ever been looked at like that in her life? She'd thought that Lawrence had cared deeply for her, but she always got the sense that he was looking just to the side of her face, beyond her. As if he was searching for more. How he'd behaved when she got pregnant proved that he'd never really seen her, let alone loved her. Everything in their lives had been like that, so she'd grown used to being enough for the moment.

Being with Ian was the opposite. He gazed deeply, searching her eyes, and when he smiled, she was overjoyed to discover he didn't seem to want anything but…*her*.

She could get used to this. Except…not with him. He was so off-limits, he might as well be wrapped in Caution tape.

But oh, what a humbling experience it'd been, seeing him lick his lips as if he was as hungry as her but *for* her as well. That she had that kind of hold over him moved her deeply. Tipped her closer to giving in than she cared to admit.

Every single thing he did nudged her closer to wanting this man, even if it was the worst idea she'd had in weeks. Months. Heck, years.

Then at dinner, she hadn't seen anything other than the date they were on. And what might happen afterward. Not her son, or the way this could complicate things if she gave in.

Because even then, she'd assumed she would

have the strength to turn away if things got too close to a real date. Now, she wasn't so sure.

Desire overrode her good sense.

Ian held her hand in his on the way back to the condo, turning it over and rubbing her palm with his thumb. It was a simple gesture, but at the same time, more intimate than anything she'd experienced in her adult life, in part because he never took his eyes off her.

"Are you still hungry?" he asked. His voice was thick and deep. This close in the cab, she was treated to his pine-scented soap that reminded her of the forest behind her new home. Oh, that she could get lost in his pine expanse…

She shook her head, even though the only competing scent in the cab was the mouthwatering lasagna they'd boxed to bring back to the condo.

"No. Not really." She wasn't, either. The bruschetta had been enough to sate her for now and leave room for…other appetites.

Don't. You should keep that barrier between you. Be friends, sure, but not more.

She only barely heard her conscience as he took her hand to his lips. He kissed each of her knuckles lightly. It was so innocent, but still felt like she was naked in the back of the cab, she was so filled with want.

The cab pulled up to the condo, and Ian released her hand so he could get out and open her door, which happened in a flash. Just as fast, they were standing in the elevator on the way to the penthouse.

Their bodies were touching from the hip up, Ian's arm wrapped around her and keeping her close. Ian's thumb rubbed her side, brushing the bottom of her breast. Whether he knew or not didn't matter. She *liked* it.

Oh, my. What the heck am I going to do when we get back? Just go to bed?

She held in a breath until the elevator dinged open to the penthouse. The chime seemed to jar him from whatever spell they were under and he released her.

Once the doors shut them in alone, Ian put the food in the fridge and then led her to the couch.

"I'll be right back. Can I get you some wine?"

Wine? Not just bed? her libido whined. But of course not. He'd come to the same conclusion she had in her saner moments this evening. Anything more than friendship was a bad idea. She didn't disagree, but that didn't mean she couldn't be a little disappointed.

"Please." He brought them both a glass and she marveled at his self-control. He didn't look at all like the same man who had demanded a to-go bag with their dinners. Instead, she watched him head to where the other bedroom was with his bag. That was it. He was setting up for a night alone, and she should, too.

She hadn't expected more, but there had been a moment she'd hoped for it.

She heard the handle rattle and got up to see what was going on.

"What's wrong?" she asked. He didn't meet her gaze, just stared at the door as he jiggled the handle. "It won't open?"

"Nope," he said. His voice was thick and lined with frustration. No doubt he was worried what that would mean.

"Can I try?" she asked. He waved her through and she gave it all she had. But no, the door was truly, 100 percent, stuck. And short of shoving through it with a shoulder, there was no way he was getting in there to sleep.

She lost it, then. Her body erupted in a fit of giggles and, at first, he just stared at her in shock.

"This is the furthest thing from funny," he growled.

That only made her laugh harder as she made her way to the kitchen. She might as well eat. "Is it?" She was leaning against the wall, then, the situation as bleak as it was hilarious. "I mean, one bed? *Really?*"

"One bed," he repeated. He growled again, wordless this time.

His eyes darkened, sobering her up. He stood over her, his scent and strength mixing like a toxin that pinned her in place. Before she could do more than nod, he pulled her against him, the overnight bag dropping to the floor.

Her gasp escaped, as did any sense of impropriety. She could pretend she was going to deny him—deny them—this. But the truth was obvious in her pert nipples and warm skin.

She wanted him and made no secret of it. His eyes scanned hers for answers, so she nodded her consent.

I'm yours, she wanted to say but couldn't. Because even if she gave into this, she couldn't be his, not really. This, if it happened, was just for tonight, nothing more. He understood. In a moment, his lips were pressed to hers and her breath was stolen. The kiss was intense, but gentle at first. When she opened her mouth, inviting him in, everything transformed into fire and ice.

Flames erupted from her chest and exploded as his tongue danced with hers. He tasted like herbs and Chianti and something uniquely his. Uniquely intoxicating. Frozen chills raced along her skin as she anticipated what would happen next.

His hand at the small of her back pulled her tighter to him so their hips were aligned. She was held up by his strength but almost turned into a puddle as he rocked into her with each thrust of his tongue.

He was huge, if the girth against her belly was any indication. He would fill her, and then some.

She moaned at the same time he lifted her onto the counter.

He kept her gaze as he held both her hands in one of his and lifted them above her head. She held her breath as he used the other hand to shimmy her top off. She sat there in her black lace bra—a luxury she'd bought hoping to use on her husband but he never seemed interested, so it'd sat in a drawer, untouched. Much like her after Henry was born.

Ian took her in and kissed along the pattern of the lace, before pulling down a swath of it to expose her hard nipple. He took it in his mouth and teased it with his tongue, then sucked all of her into his warm wetness.

"Oh, my," she whispered, wrapping her arms around him. "You know just what to do to make me—" He nipped at her with his teeth and she arched her back, quieted by desire that rocked through her.

"Make you…?" he questioned, his breath hot on her skin.

"Make me crave more of you," she whispered. He pulled her down from the counter, still in a state of undress.

The windows were open to the Seattle skyline and she didn't care. When was the last time she'd lived with abandon? As Ian brought her to the couch, sitting her down gently, she realized she couldn't recall.

"So, this is okay?" he asked, kissing her shoulder, then the crook of her elbow. Then her palm, before placing the latter on his chest.

"It is," she said. She didn't recognize her own voice, it was so tight with desire. He smiled and gently used the leverage between her arm and his chest to lean her back against the couch.

"How about this?" he asked again. This time, he held her gaze as he unbuttoned her jeans. She nodded. "And this?" He slid her jeans over her hips, no small feat since they were her snuggest pair.

"Yes," she whispered. Had she done that on purpose? Chosen an outfit that would draw *this* out in her new friend? Even subconsciously had she hoped this would happen?

Duh. Be real. He was never just a friend or colleague. You've been crushing on him the whole time.

True. But that didn't mean she shouldn't heed the warning bells in her head. Because she couldn't imagine going back to just friends, either. Nor could she picture passing him in the clinic hallways, or the blush that would ensue each time he smiled down at her.

Best not to think about that while his fingers were hooked around her lace panties pulling them down.

Fine. Do this, but it can only be for one night. Got it?

Her conscience didn't even want that, but there was no way it was intervening at this point. Not with Ian in front of her, his mouth peppering her stomach with soft kisses.

One night. I can agree to that.

Anything to keep his lips, his hands, on her. She'd have bargained away a week of vacation for this one night. It was worth it. It had to be.

Within a minute, she was clad in nothing but her black lace bra, and her legs were bent, knees open. She should feel some kind of warning, shouldn't she? Intimidation? Embarrassment at being exposed to this man she'd only known this side of a week?

But all she felt was a burning desire for him to see all of her, to touch all of her.

He licked his thumb and met her gaze, this time the question in his eyes instead of on his tongue. She nodded her silent consent, and he smiled. His thumb pressed against her tight bud and she gasped.

"Shhh," he said. "I'm going to make you want to scream my name, but I want you to put that energy back into just feeling this. Okay?"

She nodded. She felt herself get wet for him just at those words, at that single touch. He was going to unravel her, wasn't he?

When his thumb slid down the wet entrance to her sex, thrumming her before slipping a finger inside her, she had all the confirmation she needed.

"Open up for me," he told her. She found that request—made as a gentle demand—to be so dang hot. Like he wanted her enough to tell her how. Like he wanted to please her.

Oh, she was *so* here for that.

She spread her knees wider. He slipped another finger inside her folds and she bit down on her knuckles to keep from screaming out loud.

"Good job. You take direction well."

"I can be a good patient, Doctor," she teased. Maybe it was too much, too flirty, but he groaned and nodded.

"You're a perfect patient," he said, grinning up at her. They laughed together before his face dipped between her hips and his tongue joined his fingers, tracing and tasting her.

"Oh," she whispered. He hugged her hips, drew her butt to the edge of the couch and sucked and nibbled until he was right—she wanted to scream out his name from the top of the penthouse roof. When the moon rose over Puget Sound behind him, it was the last thing she noticed outside the pure bliss of coming for a man she had a serious crush on—a very secret, very temporary and forbidden crush.

When she'd finally settled down, his head lay on her chest. She played with his hair, her breathing still dysregulated.

"How the hell did you do that? I've never..." She trailed off. She had no desire to bring anyone else into this moment, but a lifetime of mediocre sexual experiences stacked in her memories. He'd vanquished their hold over her with one intimate moment. He was a darn magician.

"I am a doctor, you know." Or that, she thought, suppressing a giggle. "Anatomy class was very instructive." He kissed her abdomen, then her hip bone. "For instance, I learned that this is an erogenous zone. Am I right?"

She panted out a reply. "Yes." Then she giggled when his hands traced her sides up her ticklish zones. "Your anatomy lessons were much different from mine. I demand a refund for medical school."

He laughed heartily and hugged her tightly. It was so sweet, it almost brought her to tears.

"I'm so damn glad you agreed to come here with me," he told her.

"I thought you were asking me to come with you to observe. Maybe to assist. But that was it."

He kissed her shoulder and she didn't mind the goose bumps that erupted outward from where his lips touched her skin.

"Mmm," he whispered into her body. "I think I've wanted you like this since I met you, but this isn't my normal…thing."

She tilted his head up to meet her gaze.

"One-night stands aren't my thing either, sir."

His face paled and his smile dropped. Oh no. Had she said something wrong?

"That's not—I mean, I'm not saying…" He pulled back and she tugged him closer again. He obliged, but there was tension in his shoulders where there hadn't been any before. "I hadn't thought about what this meant. That's all. But if you—"

She kissed him. Her mouth opened in invitation and his tongue met hers, tangling with it and leaving no room for misinterpretation. Casey wrapped her arms around his neck and pulled him so that he was flush against her naked body again.

The groan of lust that traveled from his mouth to hers spoke everything she needed to hear. She had to keep her distance or they both risked ruining so much more than just this new connection. But that didn't mean they couldn't ride this amazing chemistry out tonight. After all, they'd come so far already…

"I think that's all we can do. Can we just accept this amazing night as a gift we don't want to squander, and not overthink it?" She didn't know what she wanted, but more of the thing they'd just done was on the "yes, please" list, at least until they left to go home.

What it would look like at work was something she'd let future-Casey work out.

"Sure. That sounds safe, smart." Those words—*safe* and *smart*—were like a drug to her. He kissed her deeper this time, his hands cupping her butt. "What do you want to do tonight, then?"

He nipped at her bottom lip with his teeth and she giggled. Ian at his most playful was hard to turn away, even though part of her warned that she should follow the more serious line of discussion to get it out of the way.

When he kissed the nape of her neck, breathing softly against her ear, she was a goner.

"I want you and that thing you did with your tongue, where you—"

His head was between her breasts in a millisecond, his tongue tracing the curve of them. She gasped, pleasure filling her in places that she'd just thought were overflowing. Apparently, her body recovered quickly with this man.

"This?" he asked, his breath warm on the dampness he'd lined along her skin.

"No, but I don't mind that—"

His head dipped lower still, this time to her belly button. He kissed it, then tickled the skin around it with his tongue. She writhed with desire.

"Oh, Ian—"

"You mean this, then," he said. She shook her head.

"No," she whispered. He growled and his head was between her legs as his arms pulled her knees apart, opening her up to him.

He licked her from the center of her, up to her clit. She arched her back and moaned his name in an exhale while she wrapped her fingers in his hair.

"Aha. You want more of this," he said. She glanced down at him and should have been embarrassed at the shine of her moisture on his lips. Instead, it turned her on.

"Yes," she panted.

"Tell me what you want. I need to hear you say it."

"I want that. I want your mouth on—on me."

He nuzzled her with his nose, and she didn't want him to stop. But he pulled back and leaned up on his elbows.

"Tell me what you want my mouth to do to you and if you're specific enough, Nurse Casey, I'll give you what you ask for."

She might come right then and there, just knowing she could tell him what she wanted and he'd obey. Where should she start…

"I want you inside me, I want you to make me come with this," she said, her hand cupping his erection beneath his pants.

"Oh, I think we can get a prescription for that particular therapy, but only if you're willing to work for it."

He stood and gazed down at her.

She followed the path he'd taken with her, unbuttoning his pants, then sliding those and his black boxer briefs over his hips till they pooled at his feet. She inhaled sharply. Oh, this wouldn't disappoint at all. He was hard and long enough she knew he'd fill her.

She licked her lips and tilted her head. She wanted him inside her, but there was time for that. She wanted to please him, too.

"Can I?" she asked.

He nodded that she keep going so she took him in her mouth and moved over him, slow at first, then with added pressure and speed as he groaned his approval.

"Holy—" Ian said, his fingers tangled in her curls. "You're going to make me come," he growled. "Stop, please."

He pulled back and confusion spread across her face. Had she done something wrong?

"I'm clean," he said. "I test after each new partner."

She nodded, still unsure where this was going. "Me, too. And I'm on birth control."

His smile turned on as bright as the sun reflecting off the Sound on sunny mornings.

"Good. Because I'm too old for kids and I want to make you forget I ever asked you not to scream my name."

"Yes, please." Her nervous system calmed. "I want everything you have to give me, Dr. Matthews."

Ian gathered her up in his arms, kissing her while he carried her to the bedroom.

She giggled as he set her down and lifted his eyebrows at her like he was a cartoon character.

"Careful what you wish for, Nurse Larsen."

This man, Dr. Ian Matthews, her new colleague and temporary lover, was bringing her back to herself one kiss and adventure at a time. She wasn't sure where this was taking her, but she wasn't complaining. Especially not as Ian entered her, giving her one more thing to be thankful for.

This move was turning out to be the best of her life. Hopefully, it stayed that way when they went home and she had to forget the best night of her life. Because, as she'd bargained with her conscience, she only had one night with this man, and not a moment more.

CHAPTER NINE

IAN REACHED OUT—nothing but satin expanse on the bed. No warm, soft skin, no curves he'd memorized, no gentle purring of her soft snoring.

That meant no Casey.

His eyes shot open and he glanced around the room and what he could see in the foyer. Sure enough, the bed beside him was nothing but wrinkled sheets. No woman, but proof enough he'd not dreamed up the best night of his life. He propped himself on his elbows and was treated to the detritus of their night of shared passion.

He smiled and ran a hand through his hair, which felt like the rest of the room looked. Not that he was complaining.

The lovemaking bout—all three of them, actually—certainly wasn't how he'd imagined the evening would go, but in the best way possible. If he was being honest with himself, he'd come to Seattle looking forward to getting to know Casey better, but only in his wildest dreams would he have entertained learning the depths of her the way he had.

He wanted to do anything he could to recreate that while they were still in their bubble. But she'd need to be close enough for him to do that… Where was she? The water wasn't running in the bathroom, and there weren't any sounds coming from the kitchen.

He hopped out of bed and stretched. His body felt like he'd been on an operating table for half a day, it was so stove-up.

"Casey?" he called out. He made it to the living room and discovered her asleep on the couch, a book on her chest, and clad in his undershirt from the night before. Her nipples pressed against the cotton fabric and in seconds he was half hard again, like he hadn't just spent the better half of the night before wrapped in her arms, making love to her. Her hair cascaded across her shoulders and she snored softly. She looked so peaceful, but why didn't she stay in bed with him? Was she already pulling away from him, thanks to the agreement they'd made that they only had this one night? He didn't want it to be over, though. He wanted to savor the last of the morning with her.

He gently shook her shoulder. "Casey," he tried again.

Her eyelids fluttered awake and he damn near melted when a smile bloomed on her face.

"Hi," she said, stretching. He tried to ignore the way the shirt pulled up, exposing that delicious hip muscle he'd been kissing just hours ago. But his gaze, his hands, his everything was drawn like a magnet to her skin. Especially those curves. "I woke up in the middle of the night and didn't want to disturb you, so I came out here to read. I guess I fell asleep again."

He held out a hand and she took it.

"Come back to bed," he said. He didn't pose it as a request, and she nodded. "I want every last second of that body before we—" The rest of the sentence lodged in his throat.

"I know. Me, too, Doc." She winked and stood up. The shirt barely covered her butt, and he groaned before cupping it and squeezing.

"This thing is a damned work of art, you know that?"

She laughed and it filled the room with a joviality she brought everywhere she went.

"It's actually the work of hiking and Pilates, but thanks."

"Well, I hope you don't mind, but I'm going to show it all my appreciation while we linger in bed."

She nudged him with her hip. "Aren't you tired of me yet? We spent all night with you 'appreciating' my backside."

He dragged her back into bed and covered them with the satin sheets and down comforter.

"Nope. If anything, I think whatever your lip gloss has in it should probably be labeled as a controlled substance." He kissed her long and deep, then nudged her into the crook of his shoulder. He exhaled, feeling better now that she was back beside him. Worry about what that meant for working under their one-night agreement crept across his skin like a disease. "You're addicting, you know."

She kissed his chest. "You, too."

He had an intrusive thought about her phone, something he was supposed to remind her about, but with those doe eyes fixed on him, her lips gleaming with moisture, how was he supposed to remember what it was, especially with their available minutes ticking past too quickly? He wrapped her up in his arms and pressed his lips to hers.

He liked this woman, wanted her next to him all night if it was possible. The intrusive thoughts changed course.

What if…what if they kept their one-night agreement, but extended the terms? Just casually continued what they'd started? And agreed to only physical—no actual dating that they were both averse to.

His conscience's reaction was swift. *She. Has. A. Kid. And not just any kid. He's got more needs than you're able to take on. There's no such thing as casual.*

That might be true, but he could work around Henry's challenges. In fact, arguably there weren't many people on the planet better equipped to do so.

But are you willing to take that on? To give up the life you have? You'd better be damned sure before you go there…

He couldn't answer that. He'd just gotten his sea legs back under him when it came to practicing medicine. Diving into a relationship—if that was even something Casey was interested in—probably wasn't the best idea he'd had.

Even though not being like this with her seemed infinitely less appealing than the alternative, they'd agreed to one night. That was the plan, and it made sense…even if it sucked.

His phone buzzed on the nightstand, and he looked at the clock beside it. It was ten already. He'd silenced his notifications, meaning it must be Greg or Ethan.

He swiped it up and froze. *No, no, no, no, no.*

"Casey."

She must have heard the worry in his voice and she sat up, her posture as rigid as his. He felt like a statue, unsure of what to do or say…

He just pointed to his phone.

"Who is it? Henry?"

He nodded. "He's okay," he finally got out, showing her the message on his phone, "but your mom has been trying to reach you. He's in the clinic with a fractured arm."

She snatched the phone from him and read while she shot out of bed.

She was tugging his shirt over her head, running down the hall in search of her own.

"We have to go," she shouted from the living room. He felt the panic in her voice as if it were his own. *Damn.* How had they missed the call from her mom?

A sinking feeling crawled through the sludge of memories from the evening before, when he'd been driven by a singular desire—to pleasure the woman until she cried out his name. He'd done that and then some.

But now, without that longing clouding his rational thought, he remembered. She'd needed to connect to the internet at Rich's house so she could check in with her mom about Henry.

He was supposed to remind her. Dammit. He'd had one job and he'd failed her, all so he could get what he wanted out of the night. And now, who knew what kind of pain that would create. Memories of the same pained look on the parents' faces of the boy who'd died on his table assaulted him.

No matter what the autopsy said, or what Casey thought, he couldn't be counted on when it mattered. He couldn't be the man she needed him to be.

A desperate need to fix this for her hid the ugly truths he'd just discovered about himself.

"I'll grab our stuff," he called back. "Use my phone to call your mom on the way." No way they were making a pit stop to take care of her phone, even though it was the reason this was an issue to begin with.

Ian didn't think he'd ever driven as fast as he did as he headed home to Hoodsport. He thanked whatever stars aligned that they made it safely, since he definitely pushed the limits of the truck and speed laws.

"He's at the clinic still," Casey whispered. She'd become despondent, still with shoulders strong and straight, but her heart clearly heavy. "Take me there." He nodded. "Please," she added.

"When will he be transferred to Seattle Children's Hospital?' Ian asked.

"They don't know. Moving him could make things worse, so they might just leave him with us for now, see if we can help him."

"That's a good thing. We're equipped for basic breaks in Hoodsport, and our team is the best in the nation. We'll take care of him, Casey."

She stared out the window, and he longed to take her in his arms again, to tell her that everything would be okay. But he couldn't know that.

Another thought crept in, silent and fatal.

It's not your job to comfort her, to fix this for her. You're not her person.

"I shouldn't have gone," she said. "This is my fault."

"Why do you think that?" he asked. He needed to keep her from crawling into her head where she'd been most of the past hour. If she shared her thoughts out loud, he could rationalize them with her. Show her why she couldn't have prevented this, not with anything other than a time machine.

"For thinking of myself instead of his needs. Did I tell you he had a playdate he wanted to go to, but

I was worried he'd get hurt? I had my mom take him to the safe park with the little kids. He was so bored he jumped off the top of the slide and—" She broke into a sob just as they pulled into town. They'd be with Henry in five minutes.

She bit her quivering bottom lip.

Ian shook his head and took her hand in his, but she pulled hers back. Every trace of the care and passion they'd shared was long gone. Their one night vanished into the warm air of the cab.

"No, you didn't tell me that." She was second-guessing her choice to go to Seattle. "But this was an accident, Casey. He's a kid, and kids get hurt when they play, even if their moms are nearby."

"Not Henry. He's going to get hurt, period. I can't help him heal if I'm not there. I can't hold his hand while he's crying if I'm in Seattle being selfish, right?"

His own heart was burdened with how to help Casey. What could he offer other than a shoulder to cry on? He was a single guy who had no experience with children outside a hospital. Even that had ended in disaster.

Now, with a young boy he'd come to care about in an emergency situation, he was truly torn. He could offer his professional services, but the potential for conflict of interest was so much worse thanks to his overactive libido. He waited for the familiar guilt and regret to sink in—the same feelings that had plagued him after the loss in Chicago.

But it didn't come. Try as he might, he didn't regret the time they'd shared, even though it was so short-lived. If anything, it'd changed him, lifted a veil he'd been seeing his life through.

An uglier truth surfaced, one he was trying to hide but couldn't any longer. He'd been secretly hoping there might be a way they could keep their connection going when they got back. Because what they had—that kind of chemistry and shared values? It was *special*. Maybe even worth rethinking his life choices for.

But then the world had intervened, and Casey had made it clear their one night was all they'd get. Pressure built in his chest and he struggled to concentrate. It was over before it began and he missed her. Already.

That didn't mean he agreed with her self-flagellation.

"You weren't selfish, Casey. You're there for him every minute of every day and he's still fallen, still gotten hurt, hasn't he?" She looked at him but didn't say anything to commit her feelings either way. "So don't you think you deserve to be a woman, not just a mom? Other moms get to—"

"Other moms don't have children with the same challenges Henry has. I'm a nurse and a mom and I know how to take care of him best."

They pulled into the clinic, but he wasn't going to let this go.

"Casey, please. You're a good mom and a good nurse. You're allowed—"

She opened the truck door and stepped out. Before she slammed the door on him, she shook her head.

"Don't tell me what I'm allowed to do. I messed up and I'm sorry I dragged you into it. I promise I'll be professional and talk to you about what happened between us at some point. But I need to be with Henry right now." She hesitated, then added, "Thank you for the ride."

With that, she shut the door and ran into the clinic. He put the truck in Park and followed her in. He'd do whatever they needed, including help Casey get out of her own way when the time came. Until then, he'd work on making sure her son was treated without any conflict of interest.

The staff in the clinic ignored him when he walked in and back to the surgical suites. Reese, their pediatrician, could be seen in the preoperating room with Henry. The boy's face was contorted in pain, but he nodded along with whatever Reese was telling him.

Greg was standing outside the room, his hands shoved in his pockets as Casey leaned into his chest. She was crying, and jealousy that she'd turned to his brother boiled in Ian's chest. He shoved it aside, knowing damn well this wasn't about him. That particular feeling—and the other intrusive, inconvenient feelings he'd had in the past week—were for him to work through.

"Hey," he called to Greg. He waved his brother over when Casey went back in the room with her son. "What's the prognosis?"

"He'll need surgery since the two breaks—his arm and shin—seem worse than they did originally. Transport doesn't seem possible since the break is a compound fracture. Reese doesn't have too much experience with OI, but he's mapping out a plan to perform the repair here and rod the arm so it has time to heal."

Ian rocked back on his heels. "Damn." He hesitated before he asked, "What can I do?"

Greg shook his head. "Short of doing the surgery yourself, not much. This is a touchy one. For a few reasons."

Ian nodded. He knew what his brother was referring to. Last time he'd operated on a child with OI, he'd barely made it out with his sanity intact. But this was different. A kid he cared for was on the table and he could fix it.

You don't just care for him. You care for her, too.

That was too damn true, and conflict of interest or not, he couldn't just stand by and watch both of them suffer, not when he could do something—everything—to fix it.

"I want in." He was walking back to Henry's room before Greg's hand wrapped around his biceps. He flexed, immediately on the defensive. "What?"

"Is that a good idea?" Greg asked.

"Excuse me?" Ian asked. Never in his whole career had his brother questioned his ability to perform at his job. The trust they had in one another spanned not only their surgical and patient care skills, but the knowledge that they would speak up if they felt ill-equipped or unprepared to do what was needed. "I know what happened before and I won't make that same mistake again. My arrogance burned off that day and won't be back. I can do this."

"It was never about your arrogance, or anything else you could have controlled, don't you see that?" Ian froze, his gaze fixed on his brother's. His breathing was short, air impossible to draw into his lungs. "Dammit, Ian, I should have said this to you in Chicago, but I don't think you'd have heard me if I screamed it from the helipad. You're the most competent doctor I've ever met. Myself included. I'm proud to be part of this clinic with you because I know I'm working with one of the best in the business and he's my brother to boot." Ian leaned against the wall, unsteady on his feet.

"Thanks, Greg."

"Don't thank me. Hear me. What happened in Chicago could have happened to any of us. I know it knocked you off your axis because of how Nora died when we were just kids. It's not the same, though, Ian. Not at all. Accidents happen and the one that happened to that boy was outside of your control. Except one part."

Ian braced for what might come next. He had been so close to making a breakthrough before they had learned about Henry's accident. That feeling was back—like what Greg said next might tip him over. Which direction, he couldn't say.

"We haven't talked about her, and that's on me. I should have opened that door for you when we got older, but I wasn't ready. I am, now—let's make time for it after we get this handled."

"I'm sorry, too. And yeah, I'd like that." Ian's breath stalled in his chest. The men embraced, and Ian felt his barriers crumble, as though he were falling. But he didn't land amongst the skeletons of his past, bones and mistakes jutting into his ribs.

He slid into a soft bed of promise, where his future was laid out at his feet if only he wanted to step forward and claim it.

There was peace in that. But he couldn't look that far yet. Like Greg said—not until this was handled. Plus, he was kinda hoping there was something in that future that needed someone else's input. And she'd need time and space with her son before anything else. He'd be patient.

"One more thing," Greg continued. *Uh-oh.* "I know how you feel about Casey and her son. So I just wanna ask, even though I know you've thought through the answer. You good with this? With operating on him?"

Ian nodded. "I am." How the hell had Greg sussed that out? Had he been that transparent?

"Before you even feel the need to articulate the question I can see in your eyes, it's because I know you. You might look the same to everyone else, but I've never seen you interested in anyone else, so it's obvious." He paused and Ian just stared. What could he say? "Because you're not outright denying it, lemme say congratulations. Is it sticky? Sure. She's a nurse in our practice, so it'll be awkward if it doesn't work out. But since it would take all three of our votes to reverse a hire, there's no power dynamic, no leverage one of you has over the other if you..."

"If we break up." *We'd have to be together first*, he wanted to say. But his brother was right—there wasn't an excuse *not* to try.

That was the thing—he wanted to, and was pretty sure when he'd woken up with Casey this morning and they'd kissed with the shared passion pulsing between them, that she'd wanted the same thing. Now, though, they were back to how it was before they'd met. He was a stranger.

Worse, he was someone she'd slept with who'd kept her from an important moment with her son, which made him *persona non grata*. Best not to share that with Greg just then, though. Even though all he wanted was some brotherly advice on how to process his new feelings and work through his insecurities around having them at all—including whether he was equipped to be a partner to anyone when his lifestyle was so isolating.

"So, can you operate? Sure. Is it complicated?" He shrugged.

To answer Greg's question, he nodded.

"I can see past the complications."

"Good, but are you prepared for what'll happen when you get to a sticky point in the surgery? Because it'll happen. What then? Can you put her face aside and do what you need to do for the patient?"

"Yeah. I can." He waited for his brother's response, his nerves firing.

Greg fixated his gaze, then smiled. "Alright, then go for it. I'm proud of you, brother."

Ian was proud of both of them. They had some healing to do, but at least they'd both acknowledged that aloud.

Reese came out of preop and joined them. He appeared to be happy, like a medically gifted golden retriever to Greg's more pensive German shepherd.

"What's it look like?" Greg asked him.

"Not good. Henry's leg fracture complicates things around his hips, which show evidence of a split along the anterior iliac spine. "I wish this was in your comfort zone. I could use you on this one."

Ian looked at Casey through the glass. She was hurting, that much was obvious. But he could help.

"I've been talking to Greg about that. Full transparency, Casey and I are—" He didn't know how to finish that sentence. "Well, not to kiss and tell, but we started something recently and I wanted you to know before I say this next thing." Reese just nodded. "I can and want to be in. I'll put personal things aside since it's new and make sure the patient is seen objectively." Just saying Henry's name would be too much…

Reese glanced at Greg. Before they could approach Casey, the three of them needed to vote. Greg nodded and so did Reese.

"I'm on board if you are, Greg. The kid is the most important thing here."

"I agree," Greg said. "But we're assisting."

Ian nodded. He finally exhaled. "Done. Let's run it by Casey."

Ian didn't waste time. He strode to the room, his shoulders back and confidence on full display. He couldn't—and wouldn't—give her any reason to doubt him.

Henry's room was somber and quiet. Thankfully, he was asleep, the pain medication having done quick work.

"What's the plan?" she asked, standing up and wiping away tears.

The three docs looked at one another.

"I don't have a solid approach, so I'm bringing in Ian," Reese explained.

Ian stepped in.

"Before we can start, I need your permission to treat him, Casey. If last night is going to get in the way of—"

Casey nodded. Relief flooded her features, and it took all of Ian's strength not to wrap her in a hug. She needed him in a different way right now.

"Please operate. Last night didn't mean anything. I need you to take care of him. He's all that matters." Her voice had regained its strength, but Ian could see that this was wearing on her, doing it alone. Her mother waited in the lobby, but only doctors and nurses were allowed back here.

Ian's heart slammed against his chest. Even though it hurt like hell to hear her say that, to disagree with every cell in his body, all he could do was nod. If he didn't use his years of experience and expertise to help Henry, he'd never get over the *what if*, never forgive himself. And Casey? Well, he'd be lucky if she ever looked him in the eyes again, let alone share a bed with him.

He needed to operate.

The risk of what he was about to take on was countered by the fear in Casey's eyes. He'd be fine, and so would Henry if he had anything to say about it.

So he let his feelings for her go. If there was a place for them, it had to wait.

"Okay. Let's do it, then," he said, squeezing her hand. She withdrew it, crossed her arms over her chest. He tried not to take it personally. He needed to be Dr. Matthews just then, not Ian, the man she'd slept with. He understood.

Okay, Matthews. Time to get to work. And he'd

best forget any thoughts he had about getting back to where they were last night. She'd made it abundantly clear it hadn't meant anything to her, and that whatever it'd been was long over.

All that mattered now was Henry.

CHAPTER TEN

CASEY HELD HER breath while she contemplated Ian's approach. On one hand, it was the risk she'd asked for all those years ago; if this surgery was successful, it would give Henry more stability, less chance he'd be prone to further breaks. It wasn't a miracle, but it was a chance for her son to have more of a childhood with less worry.

Yet, that was before she knew of Ian's grief, of his leaving medicine, of what it would be like to have a man like that—a man she'd have trusted with the greatest thing in her life—love her.

On the other hand, now those other morsels of knowledge haunted her. Not just that Ian had had a crisis of faith last time he'd operated on a boy with OI. That, she'd forgiven immediately. Every professional who took their or others' lives into their own hands had a case of the yips from time to time. The important thing was that he'd overcome it and knew why he'd been in that position and worked to better himself so it never happened again.

What she couldn't forget, couldn't get out of her

mind, was what she'd said to him in the office. She'd told him the night before hadn't mattered because, let's face it—she was hurting and in the dark underbelly of her own wild grief. In the blackness, she'd lashed out at a man she cared for.

And every word she'd said about him wasn't true.

Because the night before *had* mattered. Very much. It had opened her up to things she'd thought she'd never experience. Not *just* the sex, though, arguably, their connection in that department had been world-altering by itself. The way he touched her was a cross between a caress and a promise and she wouldn't ever be the same after his hands explored her. Discovered how to awaken her.

But it was so much more than that which drew her to him. It was the idea of being seen. Ian listened to her, and talked to her, too. He opened up about his own past and of course asked her questions about herself, but also Henry. He questioned and laughed and offered his thoughts. No other man—or even friend of hers—had ever known what to do with the lovely little boy in her life. Everyone but her mother ignored him entirely or became uneasy when she discussed his breaks and fractures, the things that challenged him from leading a life like most other children.

It was hard for them, she understood.

But not for Ian. He dove right in and discussed him outside of his diagnosis. His OI was and always would be a part of her son's life. But it wasn't the only thing that defined him. He was, outside of that, a little boy who loved the new dog in his life, wanted friends and sought out ways to sneak trouble. Ian saw and encouraged all of that.

And what she really liked? How he spoke to Henry directly. It was as if the two had their own language, their own relationship outside the one she was building with them, and it moved her.

It also terrified her, if she was being honest with herself. Henry was so fragile, and not just in the physical sense. Even at the young age of five, he wanted his mother to be happy. If he got attached to Ian and the man did the same thing Lawrence had—moved on from them to chase his own brand of high—Henry would be crushed.

And given the way Ian lived his life before she'd met him, there was a pretty high likelihood that would happen. Because how could she possibly expect that the man would change his mind and heart simply because he'd slept with her? She wasn't that arrogant, or hopeful.

Maybe that's why she'd lashed out that morning. To protect them both from falling for a man who was so very off-limits. They'd said one night, and even though she'd secretly hoped he'd ask for longer, for more, when Henry had been hurt, she'd taken it as a sign.

Back off.

As they wheeled Henry into surgery, though, she didn't see any sign of the man she'd slept with.

The one who'd kissed her within an inch of her sanity, the one who'd made her come not just once or twice, but four times in the few hours they'd been wrapped in one another's arms. He'd vanished, just like she'd asked and like he'd promised.

In that man's place was a competent surgeon in scrubs whose serious expression told her that her son was in expert hands. She was grateful. She needed that man—her son needed that man.

"My plan for Henry is to go in laterally and place a rod on one end of the anterior knee joint that will extend to the talus below his ankle. This will allow him to heal and remain protected from further injury at the same time. I'll do the same around the posterior side, giving him added protection. The physical therapy will be long, but since he's a child, he should recover quickly."

She'd nodded and agreed this was the best approach. What she wanted to say had nothing to do with the surgery. She wanted to apologize, to ask him if they could start over, but the man she wanted wasn't there anyway. And it was far more important that Henry get the care he needed than that she fix things with a man she'd spent a single night with.

"What about as he ages, though?" she asked, bringing her heart back to the moment in front of them. "Will the rods need to be replaced?"

Ian shook his head. "I'll be using telescoping Fassier-Duval rods that will grow as he does. Of course, we'll have to consistently monitor them, but aside from some basic mobility issues, they should give us the results we're looking for."

She'd read about those but hadn't known they were so widely used. *This.* This is what she'd wanted for her son when she'd made that original appointment for him in Chicago. That he had to endure what he had for him to get this treatment wasn't the way she'd hoped he'd be put on this program, but it was better than never.

"Thank you," she said. Her hand itched to take hold of his, but she fought the urge. It wasn't fair to him. "For this and everything."

He simply nodded and wheeled Henry into the operating room. The surgery was supposed to take six hours and at hour four, she was crawling out of her skin. Waiting wasn't doing her a darned bit of good so she snuck into Ian's office and grabbed the leash and Scout, figuring a walk would do them both good.

A gentle mist fell on the town, which wasn't surprising in the least. If anything, the sunshine they'd had recently was uncharacteristic of the Pacific Northwest, which received roughly eighty inches of rainfall each year, at least in her part of the Olympic Range.

Casey thought she'd mind, but found she kind of liked the gray mist that gave life to so much of what she loved about their new home.

If only the wind would die down. That was the

thing about spring in their part of the country. The beauty definitely came at a cost.

"Isn't it great?" she asked Scout. He cocked his head like he was contemplating her question but then lost interest when a black-tailed deer ran in front of their path. He didn't chase the animal but was on high alert after that. Casey couldn't explain it, but she felt better when Scout was with her; after meeting the dog on the day he'd saved the mountain biker, she'd gotten the sense that he was more attuned to the world than anyone she knew.

She was staring at a particular thread of hanging moss when a crash behind them startled Scout and he yelped. Casey spun around and felt the blood rush to her stomach. A tall alder was down at the start of the trail and from there it looked as if it had taken an electrical line down with it. Sure enough, her phone dinged.

Your service area has experienced a power loss, a text from her electric company read.

Wow. That was immediate. *Please let the clinic be okay*, she said, sending up the prayer to the universe and guardian spirits or angels she hoped were looking out for her son. His surgery was close to over, but at best, they had another hour left. They'd need power without interruption for the anesthesia to work. She recalled Erin saying something about a generator for this exact reason, but she couldn't recall if it came on immediately.

"Let's head back," she said, tugging the dog back

in the direction they'd just come. The dog didn't seem to mind when they turned around. "Good boy," she praised. She took off at a light jog, the dog keeping pace at her side. When they got near the downed tree, she could see the line it'd taken down with it and it wasn't good. It was snapped in two places, so she steered them away from the danger.

Scout wouldn't budge, though. He whined and pulled toward the base of the tree.

"Scout, come," she tried, but the dog pulled and wouldn't relent. "What is it, boy?" She finally gave in and let him lead the way, trusting that, with his save from before, he sensed something amiss.

He was right. Behind the tree was another, wider tree that had fallen—from the looks of it because of the rain soaking the ground and the wind whipping through the evergreens. Trapped under one of its large branches was a small motorcycle and its rider.

"No," she whispered. There was no way through the area from the south, which is where emergency medical services would come from. She'd need to get help from the clinic, but with Henry in surgery and her unable to assist, they were already short-staffed. Too bad. This rider needed help right away and she didn't have more than one bar of service on her cell phone. She let it continue to dial the clinic, in the hopes it would go through. But she couldn't rely on that alone.

She released Scout's leash from his collar and pointed to the clinic.

"Get Erin," she said. "Get someone from the office, boy," she instructed. Scout gave a yip like he understood her and tore off in the direction of his new home. It was a risk to send for help by way of an animal, but what choice did she have?

She approached the rider and winced. The man had a helmet on, thank goodness, because he'd been tossed not only into the road, but onto a boulder alongside it. His shoulder looked dislocated at first glance and his arm dangled limp at his side. Worse, though, was his leg. Like with Jeff, the mountain biker, it was broken in what looked like two places, but one of them was a compound fracture.

It would need surgery as soon as Ian was done with Henry's bone set and rod placement.

She took a knee and assessed the rider's situation. His foot was caught under the weight of the downed tree, which meant he'd need to be cut out and the foot would need work as well.

Darn it. What horrible luck to be riding under a tree just as it fell. What was the rider doing out in the rain like that, anyway? And on such curvy roads?

She checked the rider's airway, careful not to move him until they could assess whether he'd broken a vertebra in his neck or back. He was breathing, but it was shallow. She kept a finger on his pulse and counted while she waited for her phone call to go through.

That was the thing about these kinds of risks.

Sure, there was an element of thrill in the likelihood that you could be in danger in pursuit of fun. But when that inherent danger became a reality, all bets were off. Risk was just risk and hurt was the only outcome.

The sound of an engine in the distance brought hope with it.

Please be someone who can help. She didn't know who'd been called into surgery for her son and thinking about that added to her anxiety. She wanted to be back in the clinic, to know the power was on and that everything was fine with Henry.

She squinted in the rain, rivulets of water running down the bridge of her nose and into her mouth. Being this close to the sea meant the rain had a hint of salt in its belly. She could only see the outline of the truck, which was indistinguishable, but the shape that jumped from the driver's seat and ran toward her she'd know anywhere.

Ian.

"Over here," she called out when he first went to the smaller tree that was more visible. "Ian!"

That got his attention, and he sprinted to her side in mere seconds with a medic bag and…was that a chain saw? She'd never been so happy to see anyone in her life.

But if he was there—

"Henry's in recovery," he said, answering her unasked questions while he did his own assessment of the accident scene. "He did great and things went faster than Greg or I expected. We were just coming out to get you when Scout showed up."

Every cell in Casey's body wanted to cry, to jump for joy. Her boy was okay. But the motorcyclist wasn't, and until he was, she couldn't relax.

"Thank you. And thank you for coming. Is there power?"

"There is. Generator didn't skip a beat, nor should it have with how expensive that sucker was."

"Thank goodness," Casey said. "How did you know where I was?"

Ian pointed to the passenger side of the truck where Scout sat stalwart in the cab.

"That guy. He barked at the entrance until Erin met him and we realized you weren't there. I was actually so scared—" He trailed off, his gaze pinned to hers, and she blanched.

"Oh," she whispered as understanding dawned on her. Of course he would think it was her that was hurt. What was she thinking? "I'm sorry. I'm also sorry for…for earlier."

She didn't elaborate and he didn't ask any questions.

"It's okay. Let's take care of this guy and then I'll fill you in on Henry." She nodded, glad for the change in topic. Gosh, how she wished it could be different for them, but as usual, different meant she wouldn't have the son she had and that was not anything she'd entertain.

Ian started up the saw to remove enough of the tree that they could lift it off the rider.

Casey cut back his clothes, but only after setting up a tarp from the bag as a makeshift shelter. "We don't have a sterile field, so we should think about transporting him," she said as he removed the branch of the tree from the patient. Sure enough, the foot looked like it had been crushed.

Ian agreed and taped up the rider's foot while she held him still. He was still unconscious but Ian ruled out any immediate danger outside of his fractures. The compound was by far the worst, but even that could be repaired with minor surgery. The man had gotten as lucky as he could for an event like this. Including his rescue.

"You know," he said, walking around and clearing debris from the area so they could move him, "this is Scout's second rescue. I think we really ought to put him on payroll."

"That's true." She grabbed as straight a stick as she could find and handed it to him in case he was in search of a splint. "What do you need me to do?" she asked.

"Can you place the splint?" She nodded and began. "That's perfect," he told her. The praise was so genuine from him. "Okay, this next part is gonna suck," he said. "I'm gonna need you to help me move him into my truck so we can get him to the clinic."

After the splint was placed, they used the tarp

from their shelter to carry him to the truck where Scout awaited them like the trooper he was.

"How did he lead you here?" she asked.

"He barked each time I almost made a wrong turn until this street, then he just whined. I was so glad to hear your voice, you don't even know."

She didn't know what to say to that last part. "He's such a good boy," she commented. Gosh, what she wouldn't give to have Scout around for Henry, to see when her son might need something. What a gift that would be.

"I meant to tell you that I asked Greg the other day if Scout could stay with you or I since he's always on the go to the city, and he said that would be best. What do you think? Would Henry be okay with a dog around to help his recovery?"

"I was just thinking about that. I think he'd love it," she said. It amazed her how well this man could read her questions before she articulated them.

"Good. Let's talk to Greg when we're back and settled. I'll help any way I can, Casey." She believed him, too. That was the thing about Ian. She could trust him implicitly; such a difference from how she'd felt with Lawrence. But was that enough? Could she trust that he would tell her if he needed more instead of just leaving for longer and longer adventures until one day he disappeared altogether?

She'd like to think so, but experience wasn't in her favor. As much as she liked this man, she needed to play it safe with him.

At the clinic, the motorcycle patient was handed over to Greg, and Casey was instructed to go be with her son. She wanted to follow through with helping Ian on this latest case, but there was nothing on the planet that could keep her from Henry at this point.

Erin and Reese helped get Casey home for some rest while Henry recuperated in the clinic. She'd had half a mind to crash with him at the clinic—she was so bone-tired—but her new colleagues had insisted Henry needed her to be rested. She reluctantly agreed. She got out her phone and texted Ian a message.

Thank you, it read. She sent that off, then realizing how paltry an offering that was, she started on a second one.

What you did for me, and for Henry in there today is a gift I'll never be able to repay. I know you said you didn't want to treat him, that you were done with that part of your life, so that you stepped up when we needed you will be something I'll carry with me every day of my life. Henry will, too. In fact, when he woke up just before I left, he was groggy, but he asked about you. Then he told me he wanted to be a doctor like you.

She hit Send again and cringed as she reread it. She'd undersold the first one and overshot the second.

Sorry for the long text. All I meant to say was thank you. I'm more grateful than you'll ever know.

She was pretty sure there was a rule about double-texting men before they wrote you back, and if that was the case, then triple-texting was a definite no-no. But oh, well. She'd messed up any chance of seeing where they could go romantically, but maybe they could have a chance at being more than just colleagues. At this point in her life, she'd settle for having a good friend.

Casey's mom came in just as she closed her phone down. Casey shot her a smile.

"Thanks, Mom. I'm so sorry that happened on your watch. I should have been here."

"No apologies needed. I'm just glad he'll be okay." Her mom waved her off and pointed at Casey's phone. "He's a good one, you know. One you don't have to worry about."

Pretending not to know what her mom meant wasn't possible—not without risking a deeper conversation at the other end—so she just nodded.

"I know."

Her mom didn't say much else, just kissed Casey's head and went to bed. Before she could muster the energy to do the same, the front door camera alert on her phone activated, showing a man in a ball cap.

Ian?

Had he come by to check on Henry? It was almost nine o'clock—who else could it be?

She hopped up and smoothed her hair.

Her stomach churned with nerves as she pretended to walk calmly to the door. She ran through a list of things she wanted to tell him, apologies she wanted to make, but when she peeked through the window, no one was there.

She opened the door in spite of her confusion. The stoop was empty, save for a package. It must have been a delivery person who'd rung the doorbell. She took the box inside, noting that it was addressed to Henry, care of her.

Curious, she opened the box and read the letter on top.

Dear Henry,

You were so brave and strong today. I'm feeling pretty lucky to have met a little champ like you. Thanks for trusting me to fix your leg—hopefully this will last a long time, and you'll be back to playing before summer hits. Until then, while you're healing, I heard you're reading big kid books now, with chapters. These were my favorite, so I hope you enjoy them. If not, tell your mom and I'll bring something different. Stay cool, and see you soon. —Dr. Ian

Casey's heart squeezed in her chest. She was pretty sure, if she were hooked up to monitors, that she'd see a rapid uptick in her pulse as she sifted through the books.

There were ten of them, all stories she recalled from her own childhood about four orphaned siblings who lived in a boxcar and adopted a dog that accompanied them on all their adventures.

It was so perfectly Henry that Casey wept. In part because her son was so clearly seen by this man, a first in his experience.

She also felt each tear as an apology to Ian for how horribly she'd treated him today. She hadn't meant to snap at him. The weight of what she carried on her son's behalf was heavy, but Ian had shown her she could put it down from time to time.

The thing was, she wasn't used to that, and wasn't sure she could trust that he'd pick it up in the same way she would.

She put the box on the other side of her bed, where a partner would be if she had the heart to let one in. But who would want to come into this world, in and out of hospitals and stacked with fear about every movement, every twist her son made?

The books were a nice gift—the most thoughtful one she'd ever received on behalf of her son. But she couldn't trick herself into thinking it meant anything. She might have been out of line saying the night before hadn't meant anything, when it had to her, but maybe it was best to keep moving on.

Then, no one—not Henry, not her, not Ian—could get more hurt than they already were if he couldn't commit the way she and Henry would need him to…in a way Lawrence never could.

That was her last conscious thought as she drifted off to sleep, craving the comfort of the man's arms that had held her just hours ago. The man who was the reason she'd come to Washington.

That couldn't factor in. She had to forget him.

CHAPTER ELEVEN

IAN CLEARED HIS throat and knocked on the door with the hand that wasn't full. In the other, he delicately balanced a bottle of wine, a bag with a surprise for Henry—who had made such incredible progress he'd been sent home earlier than anyone expected, Ian included—and some handpicked daisies from Ian's hike along Hurricane Ridge that morning.

What the hell am I doing here? He wasn't sure, only that doing something was better than nothing.

He wouldn't be there at all if Casey's mom hadn't suggested it when he'd stopped by Henry's room on his rounds. He'd missed Casey each time he'd visited, but her mom was kind and generous in her time with Ian and alluded to the fact that her daughter could use a break—and Henry could use some…freedom from her worry.

That suited Ian, too.

The past three days, he'd been crawling out of his skin hoping to get a chance to talk to Casey but didn't want to reach out if she was actively avoiding him. A thank-you text was one thing—but that had been it. No calls. No way of knowing if she was okay. He understood that she needed the time off to care for Henry, but who was taking care of her while her mom worked? He'd fought against his inner critic that kept reminding him that wasn't his job.

I want it to be, though.

He'd felt like the walls were closing in on him at home, so he'd ducked out and done a quick ten-miler through the park while he contemplated if he should go to Casey's.

The birds were chirping, the sun broke free from its morning foggy shawl after mile three, and his legs worked in his favor, churning him up the steep path as if he was electronically powered. He couldn't have asked for more.

That'd been the impetus to break the radio silence and reach out to her. He knew Henry was good, but he wanted to make sure she was, too.

So, he'd asked Casey's mom if she could be there that evening and in addition, when her next day off was. Both Casey and her mom didn't work Friday, so he'd booked the spa treatments and made sure they were flexible with cancellations. Casey might not want him, which he'd see either way in the next few minutes, but she still deserved a break and to be cared for.

The door opened and he could tell his visit was truly a surprise. He hadn't specifically asked

Casey's mom to keep his visit to herself one way or another, so he wasn't sure what he was expecting. But it was amazing to see Casey without pretense or thinking too much about what she needed to do or show up as.

She wore a plain white tank top with spaghetti straps and gray sweatpants, her hair tied back in a simple knot that left a few strands free. Her face was fresh, no makeup or anything to distract from her natural beauty.

He gulped nothing but air since his mouth had gone dry. She was stunning. And also staring at him like he had three heads.

"Hi," he started. *Lame*, his heart whined. *You can do better.* "I missed you and hoped I could convince you to take a break. Not as my lover, or whatever path we were on, but as a friend like we said we wanted. You've made it clear you don't want more, but I don't want to lose you all together. Can we start over, please?"

Better.

The soft smile that shone through the clouds in her expression said she agreed. He handed her the flowers. She accepted and smelled them, her smile growing wider.

"They're beautiful, thank you."

"They're from the ridge. I'd love to take you there sometime soon." He stopped himself when her brows raised high enough they almost met her hairline. "Not today, obviously. I was hoping for something…more mellow today. Something that'll allow you to let off steam without exhausting you. What do you say?"

"I can't take a break since I'm alone, but…would you like to see Henry? He's been asking about you since we got home yesterday. I think he'd like to talk about the latest adventure of those kids in the boxcar. He's been reading them nonstop."

"I'm glad he likes them and I'd love to say hi to the little man. But did you say you're alone?" Her mom was supposed to relieve Casey—that was the only way his plan worked.

She led him inside and he put the wine on the counter, but held on to his bag. "Yeah, through tomorrow evening." Her smile wavered and he saw the exhaustion under her eyes. Had her mom gotten the day wrong? Had he? Worry flickered across his mind about how he'd pivot if she didn't show.

It wasn't a hard sell for his imagination. He'd open up the gift he'd brought Henry and crack the wine he'd bought for Casey's mom as a thank-you, pouring Casey a nice glass while he drew her a bath. Hell, that almost sounded as good as or better than what he'd already drummed up. Hopefully, there would be time for that too someday, though.

If he was being honest, he'd thought of a dozen things he wanted to do with Casey and the list kept growing. This was gonna be a problem if she didn't want anything to do with him, especially since, now that he was a little open to the idea, she didn't seem to want anything to do with him in that way.

Maybe he should take it as a sign that her mom hadn't shown up, and let Casey—and her hold over him—go.

In answer to that, the door burst open and Casey's mom walked in, breathless and windswept. "I'm here," she announced, grinning like she'd won a prize. Ian laughed.

"Perfect timing," he said. "I was just trying to convince your daughter to take a break."

"It's a requirement," her mom added, winking at Ian.

"Mom?" Casey asked. She glanced between the two of her houseguests, but neither offered an explanation. "What's going on?" she asked finally.

"I'll take this," Ian said. "I asked your mom if she was free to come by so I could take you to do something out of the house." She opened her mouth as if to refuse him, but he put up a hand to stop her. He wasn't—nor did he want to be—in the habit of asking her to be quiet, but he knew what her worry was. "Before you tell me this happened because you left, because you were too strict, or whatever, I have an answer to that. He won't be in danger, and he and your mom don't have to go anywhere for him to have a little adventure as well."

He pulled out the surprise for Henry.

"What is this?" she asked, turning over the box in her hands.

"It's a virtual reality headset and game console. It has games that will allow him to see the world from a first-person point of view. I brought some sports and other athletic games, racetracks and even one that lets you feel like you're a bird flying over different parts of the world. They all looked like things Henry said he wanted to try someday. Maybe this'll keep him from getting bored and let him experience those things he might not in the same way as other people."

Casey stared at him, her mouth opening and shutting twice before she just shook her head. He couldn't tell what she was thinking, but he rarely saw her lost for words.

"It's perfect, and I know he'd love that," she whispered and tears lined her eyes. He didn't mean to make her cry. "But I can't—it's too much," she protested. But the glow in her eyes said he'd hit the mark.

"You can and should. Let it be a guilt gift for pulling you with me the day Henry fell. It's also a nice way for me to spend some of Seattle Memorial's money they pay me for doing what I would do for free anyway. You'd really be doing me a favor." She seemed to consider it, rolling it over in her hands. "And it'll keep Henry entertained for hours in a safe, controlled environment. I'll argue later why that shouldn't be the only case, but for now, it's his best option for his healing. What do you say? Can I set it up for him while you get ready for our date? I mean, our time as friends?"

He corrected himself, but the flush on her cheeks made him curious. He wanted to hope there was still a chance for them, but at the same time, didn't want to live with the disappointment of trying for that, only to be pushed aside each time something else came up. He'd rather just be her friend.

That was safer for him, either way. Because even though he'd come a long way toward thinking about what it was he wanted at this stage of his life, and that Casey might be part of it, he wasn't sure what limitations hid behind his insecurities around risk.

And relationships? They were a lot of risk. The rewards were bountiful, too, like the views at the top of a rocky climb that almost killed him getting up, but they weren't guaranteed.

Like the way she was looking at him now. He couldn't figure her out, but he was still standing there, so that had to count for something.

"I'm not saying yes yet, because I need to talk to Henry and see if he is okay with me leaving," she said. He waited, his heart pattering out a tattoo of hope. "But if he agrees, what are you proposing?" she asked.

He inhaled a deep breath filled with possibility. She hadn't sent him packing yet.

"I'd like to take you across on the ferry, since it's beautiful out, and do a hike with you on Bainbridge. It's nothing technical, so you don't have to worry."

"That actually sounds amazing," she whispered. "I've heard lovely things about that part of the Northwest."

"And I already talked to Henry. He's excited for some time alone with me, so you go get ready," her mom said, shoving her daughter toward her room.

Casey looked back once and whispered, "Thank you."

When she was gone, Ian high-fived her mother and told her he was going to see Henry. He found he missed the little guy—his unfettered joy, the way he talked about his interests… He was a cool kid.

Ian walked to the back, stopping at the door to Henry's room. He knocked.

"Come in," a small voice called out. Ian was always in shock when he remembered how young the boy really was. His personality and maturity were beyond his years, something he didn't often see in OI kiddos. Most of the time, the ways they were protected by parents meant they were sheltered from the world at large, too. He had to say he appreciated the way Casey gave her son access to the world, even knowing he might not be able to engage fully in it the way other kids might be able to.

He pushed open the door to see the boy curled up in a bed shaped like a race car and Scout at his feet. The dog had more or less moved in permanently with Casey and Henry. From what Casey shared with Greg, who was overjoyed the dog had found a good home, Scout had turned into quite the rescue and service animal. Greg told Ian that when Henry needed to use the bathroom on his first night home, Scout had run to grab Casey without Henry asking him to.

Ian witnessed that for himself as Scout came to greet him, then went and nudged Henry, who hadn't looked up from his book. The boy petted the dog on the head and gave him a kiss before raising his head to meet Ian's gaze.

"Ian!" he shouted. He looked like he might pop out of bed and run to him, and then a shadow passed over his face when he realized he wasn't able to. "Sorry, I can't come say hi."

Ian shook his head. "I don't need you to. I brought you something."

"A present?" Henry asked. His eyes were bright again, and in that way, he was a quintessential five-year-old kid.

"Yep. Something I wish they'd have had when I was lying in bed with a broken leg."

Henry's expression of childish shock was almost comical, it was so pronounced.

"You've broken a leg, too?" He seemed happy to hear that, and Ian knew just why. It made him "normal."

Ian nodded. "Sure did. Twice. Turns out soccer isn't as easy as it looks, and I didn't learn my lesson either time. By the time I stopped playing, I'd broken my tibia twice, my collar bone once and a finger three times. And each time I was forced to stay home and heal, I read every book in my house. They're cool and all, and I wanna talk to you about that series since it seems like you're almost done. But I also think you need a break. What do you say?"

Henry nodded with exaggerated enthusiasm only a kid could pull off.

"Okay. Let's get this out. Have you heard of virtual reality?" he asked.

Henry nodded so hard, even Ian worried this time he might hurt himself. "VR? Heck yeah!" He clapped a hand over his mouth. "I'm not supposed to say *heck*," he whispered.

Ian bit back a smile. "I won't tell your mom," he said, winking at Henry. He gave an exaggerated wink back—or more a blink, but it was so cute Ian couldn't correct him. "Okay, so this VR set is kinda cool, and I don't mind admitting I think I brought over the perfect games now that I've seen your room."

There were posters of soccer players, race car drivers, astronauts and rock climbers littering the boy's walls. All challenges aside, he looked like any other kid with heroes and goals. In his own way, he'd conquer them.

He set up the console and taught Henry how to operate it.

"How is your leg feeling today?" he asked. He felt Henry's pulse and it was steady.

"Good," Henry said. "It hurts but I'm okay. This happened before, so I'm used to it," he said. Ian nodded. It would keep happening throughout the kid's life, but hopefully, with Ian's interventions, the breaks would be less severe and more infrequent.

"I also heard you might want to be a doctor someday."

Henry nodded as he inspected the headset. "I wanna help people like you do. People like me."

Ian's heart pounded beneath his chest. This kid…

"You're pretty amazing, Henry. You know that?"

"My mom tells me that all the time. I'm glad someone cool like you thinks so, though." Henry shrugged.

There really wasn't an end to his adorableness, was there? Something nagged at Ian, something semi-familiar. When Henry reached for his hand to adjust himself on the bed, Ian figured it out.

He wanted more of this. Of being able to be around to care for these two. They were so special, and the way he felt around them? A blend of comfort and passion? Hell, not even a run up a mountain peak with panoramic views of the ocean in the distance compared. Damn, he hadn't felt the need to go on a wild adventure since he'd met Casey. A hike, sure. A bike ride? Maybe. But nothing had compared to spending time with her.

What's that mean for you? For your hobbies?

He didn't know, but as Henry got his first game

up and running—a car-racing game—he didn't care. Henry giggled and screamed as the race picked up pace.

"I can see the finish line," he shouted. Ian laughed. Henry didn't know he was yelling over the headphones, and Ian wasn't going to be the one to tell him. "I'm gonna win!"

Three minutes later, Henry squealed with delight and ripped the headset off.

"I did it," he said, breathless.

"Congrats, bud. That's fun, isn't it?"

Henry smiled so wide, Ian could see his molars. "It sure is. Guess what?"

"What's that?" Ian asked, inspecting the cast and immobilizing device.

There was even a sheen of sweat on Henry's brow, yet the whole time he'd played, he hadn't moved his leg once. That part of Ian's treatment plan seemed to have worked—the whole world at Henry's fingertips without him straining the leg. What Henry didn't know yet was that Ian had bought games that would eventually be used as physical therapy for the healing leg. They would also build strength in other vulnerable places where Henry was prone to injury.

"There were people in the crowd with my name on signs. Isn't that the coolest? And everything was going so fast by me. I love this, Ian. Can I do another one?"

Ian laughed. "As long as your mom says it's okay, you can play as many as you want."

"Thanks, Dr. Ian. I mean it. The books are neat, but this is way cooler."

Ian laughed. "Fair, but you'll have to stick with the books, too. Adventure is fun, but it's not the whole thing. You need balance, okay?"

"Okay, Dr. Ian."

"You can just call me Ian."

Ian's phone notified him that his group chat had set a new hike for Sunday but he ignored it. He followed the group for beta on good climbs, but hadn't joined them on one yet. Right now, he wasn't even sure he wanted to take on this new route. All he actually wanted? More moments like this. He'd be fine with video games and books with this cute family for the foreseeable future.

That feeling only intensified when Casey came in. She'd changed into tights and a hiking top that showed off tan, strong shoulders he'd seen draped across his chest recently. He didn't linger there—not when she'd made it clear she didn't want him in that way. But damn if his body didn't betray him at that moment. It wanted her, plain and simple. Would that ever fade? He didn't think so—if anything, the feelings grew stronger each time he saw her.

"It's fine with me," Casey said, picking up the goggles and trying them on. The wanting her remained as she put her hands in front of her, swiping at things only she could see. "Wow. That's quite the setup. Did you say 'thank you'?"

"I did. I also said 'heck' but I don't want Dr. Ian—I mean Ian—to hide it for me. Sorry, Mom and Ian."

Casey grabbed Ian's hand and squeezed it. Both of them hid smiles from Henry. Ian felt heat and desire as he held her hand in his. But that was only on his side. She didn't feel the same way. It was alright—he'd take what he could get.

"It's fine, hon. We're gonna head out now, okay? Grandma is here if you need anything and we'll be back soon—"

"*M-o-o-m*," Henry whined. "I'm fine. I'm not a baby."

She nodded and took her hiking pack. "You got it, mister. But only an hour on this, then you have to take a break, okay?"

"Okay. Then maybe another hour after lunch?" Henry put his hands together like he was pleading for a stay of execution. Ian watched with a blend of pain and joy. In another world, this is what the kid he'd operated on in Chicago would be doing. Playing, laughing, testing boundaries…

It broke Ian's heart that his patient in Chicago would never have moments like this, but Ian had learned what he needed to so he could help Henry. He didn't take that lightly.

"You ready to get out of here?" he asked. Casey took his hand and led him to the foyer after saying goodbye to her mom and passing on the instructions for Henry's screen time. Once they were outside, Casey wheeled on Ian.

Before he could make sense of it, she'd risen up on her toes and pressed her lips to his. He melted when her hands wrapped around his neck, pulling him into her. What had it been? Five days? He kissed her back like her lips were oxygen and he'd been deprived of breathing for that long.

"Thank you," she whispered to him. Their foreheads were pressed together, their breath mingling between them. He was hard enough that if he didn't get a grip, driving would be interesting. "What you did for Henry was the single best thing anyone's done for us in a long time."

"Is that why you kissed me? To thank me?"

She laughed and shook her head. "I kissed you because I wanted to. Poor timing that I also wanted to say thank you. Sorry."

"Mmm," he said, kissing her forehead and cheeks. "No apologies if this is okay with you. It's all I've wanted since Seattle."

"I want to apologize for that," she countered. "For not saying sorry in person and for avoiding you. I thought it was best if I kept my distance after what I said. And Henry needed me, so it was easy to avoid you. Well, not easy… It was actually the hardest thing. But after what I'd said—" He simply kissed her while he nodded his appreciation. "I didn't mean that our night together wasn't the best thing to happen to me since Henry, because it was. I just—"

"You were hurting." She nodded, biting her bottom lip. He took it in his mouth and sucked on it until she moaned with pleasure.

He cupped her cheeks in his hands and parted her lips with his tongue. Their soft plumpness was so alluring, so singularly her, that it drove him to distraction.

He pulled back, something he'd been meaning to talk to her about trapped on his tongue. If he didn't say it soon, he'd lose his will to.

"I need to talk to you about Henry's case," he told Casey, breathless. "Before we do this."

"Is he—" she said, pulling back. He held her waist so she didn't go far.

"He's fine. He's great, actually. And I want to keep it that way, so I think I'd like a colleague from med school on board to take over for me as his primary physician, okay?" Her brows pulled tight in concern. "But hear me loud and clear—this isn't me abandoning him. The opposite, actually. If I get things my way, I'll be around a lot more with Henry's day-to-day and can care for him that way, but his medical care should be overseen by someone who isn't kissing Henry's mom."

Her concern melted into a smile. "I think that's a great idea. Because I still want to kiss you," she told him. "And I would like you around more. A lot more."

He laughed.

"Same here. So, I'll make it right on my end, okay?"

"Thank you, Ian. For everything."

"Shh." He smiled and helped her get into the passenger side of his truck. "We're going to be okay. Henry will be okay. Now, let's go play while we still have the daylight." She nodded and took his hand over the gearshift console.

"Yes, please, Doc," she said. His erection didn't go anywhere as they headed toward the ferry along the highway. When her hand migrated to his lap, cupping him above his hiking pants, he growled with feral desire.

"We're gonna make a pit stop," he said. She nodded.

"I was hoping you'd say that."

Yeah, Ian thought as he pulled over just ten miles into their trip to a secret lookout he knew about from his last season of climbing. *I could get used to this.*

His heart warned that it was too soon, that there was a lot at risk here—more so than any climb he'd completed in his life. He ignored it, though, because this felt too damn good to consider any other possibility. He liked this woman and wanted her and the life she offered—no matter the risk.

He might regret that someday, but not today.

CHAPTER TWELVE

EVERY ADMONITION CASEY had given herself when it came to Ian flew out the open window of the cab of his truck. Her hair blew in the breeze as they drove onto the street that led to the ferry. This was their second trip to Orcas Island since the hike in Bainbridge after Henry's surgery. What Bainbridge lacked in rural charm, Orcas made up for. Same with the sense of adventure in the mix of land and sea. It was quickly becoming one of her favorite places outside the Olympic Range.

Ian was just as quickly becoming one of her favorite people. He'd somehow, effortlessly, found a way past her defenses, lowering them with each kiss, each lovemaking session, each hour he spent playing on the VR set with Henry or reading her son a book…

Each adventure like this one made her feel more and more like she was coming back to herself.

He'd extricated himself from Henry's care, which he'd transferred to Dr. Holm in Seattle. He was a fabulous pediatric orthopedic surgeon and Henry loved his office, which, of course, was decorated in octopuses—an "orthopedic marvel" as Dr. Holm called them.

Ian had even brought her mom some joy with the spa day he'd booked for the ladies. They'd gone for facials, massages and a series of plunges in hot, cold and tepid waters and then out to dinner together. She'd waxed poetic about the man to Casey, and even let Casey set her up with a social media dating site.

"If there are men like this out there," her mom had said, "why wouldn't I take the risk and get back out there?"

That risk was never far from Casey's thoughts, even when she was relaxing by the pool of the spa. It'd felt good to put her worries down, and not just leave them there for her to tend to when she returned. No, Ian had taken such good care of Henry, she hadn't had to worry all day. About him at least. All the while Casey and her mother were at the spa, Ian had taken Henry in his new wheelchair to the aquarium and then out to dinner at her son's favorite spot—the Rainforest Café. He loved the calls of the birds and roar of the jungle cats.

She also knew he loved the desserts that, of course, Ian had splurged on for them both. That day had been so magical for so many reasons, partly because Henry had had such a good time, but also because Casey really couldn't recall the last time she and her mother had been alone together without

Henry in tow. If they were, who would she trust to take care of her most precious cargo?

That was the part of the worry that hadn't gone away, though—her fear about what this all meant for her heart. Because it was so fully invested, she didn't think she'd ever get it back in one piece if they stopped whatever it was they were doing.

Which, at the moment, was holding hands and preparing to try out a new trail that Ian had found from his buddies who did this sort of thing all the time. Her mom was encouraging her to get out more, and she was—but not without the cost of some heavy mom guilt. She tried to let it go, but it was hard.

Equally as hard was wondering what Ian was thinking about them. Did he miss his old way of life? Because the types of hikes he took her on were mere shadows of those he used to conquer. While the trails they hiked were steep, they were also out-and-backs or loops that spanned two or three hours instead of days or weeks. He'd skipped out on a climbing trip because Henry had needed to be taken to physical therapy, and Casey was working and her mom had been called in to work as well. He'd volunteered and, short of any other option, Casey had accepted, but he'd not said more than "no problem" when she'd asked if there was anything she could do to make up for what he'd missed out on.

More guilt piled on the already high hill of the stuff accumulating at her feet.

"Can I ask you something?" she wondered aloud, biting her lip with worry.

"Are you wondering if we can stop for ice cream on the way back?" he asked. "Because it's already in the plans." He winked at her and her heart rate increased. This man knew just how to elicit a spike in her numbers. A simple touch or glance or kiss… oooh. That last one always undid her.

"Don't threaten me with a good time, Doc." She laughed nervously, the words stuck to the roof of her mouth. "But no, that's not what I was going to ask."

"Okay, shoot. You can ask me anything."

She took a deep breath, the sea air thick and calming. The question took a moment to form, but finally it came to her in two parts. *The only way to it is through it*, she figured, and launched in.

"Do you miss your old life? The one before Henry and I? Which I guess begs a second question." She paused and he nodded that she continue. *I can do this. The worst he says is that he doesn't want me like I want him. And isn't it better to know now?* "What are we doing? I mean, are we dating? Like, are we a couple? Henry's asked about us, and I'm not sure what to tell him. Do you even want to be more than friends who kiss?" Ian smiled and pulled over on a dirt road that looked deserted.

"Where are we going?" she asked.

"That was more like five or six questions, but as fate would have it, I brought you to Orcas Island today because I want to show you something that might help answer some of those questions—and some bigger ones."

"Are we about to do that thing we did last week?" she asked, referring to when she'd slipped a hand between his boxers and skin while he drove and teased him until he couldn't stand it any longer. He'd pulled over, much as he'd just done, parked, and in one swift movement he'd unbuckled her seat belt and had her sitting atop him. They'd made love there, then later in the bed of the truck over a view that included a breathtaking scene of boats below them in the harbor. It was lovely, but not what she was looking for at that particular moment. "Because you showed me that twice since, and while I love it, I really do think we need to talk about this."

He smiled, yet he didn't slow down until they reached a field that opened up to a quaint little bay with a few buildings along its coast. He pulled up and parked where they had a view of the activities below.

"What is this?" she asked. There were kayaks dappling the sun-stained water, each with kids at the helm. Swimming in the right side of the bay were snorkelers, all with vests on to ensure they floated. They were all kids, too. "Is it a summer camp?" she asked. The kids splashed and laughed and genuinely sounded like they were having a lovely time. A stab of jealousy at how much Henry would love a place like this rammed between her ribs.

He grinned like the day he'd summited Hurricane Ridge with her. It'd been hard, but his pride was worth each excruciating step. She was getting her hiking and sea legs back, it seemed.

"It is. It's for kids with OI, like Henry."

Her skin went clammy and suddenly the breeze off the Salish Sea felt cold. She shivered and rolled up her window. The cab was suddenly quiet.

"Why did you bring me here, Ian?" she asked. This was one question she didn't want him to answer, though, because the ideas of what he'd say terrified her. In fact, he still hadn't answered any of her other questions.

"I hope we can talk about bringing Henry here this summer. He's the right age and all the staff are doctors trained to work with kids with challenges related to osteogenesis imperfecta. It's kinda like a cooler, water-based camping version of what we do in Hoodsport," he said.

She nodded but it was robotic, automatic. "Yes, but why?"

He took her hand, and she flinched but didn't pull hers away. With the windows shut, she felt claustrophobic.

"Because he loved the aquarium, so I started looking at ways he could have a little adventure, but with some safety nets in place. This place popped up in my search and I came up to interview the docs and staff. It's legit, Casey. Henry would be safe here."

She ran a hand through her hair, and it caught on a tangle. Tears sprang to her eyes.

"Where would I be?" she wondered. She'd never spent more than twenty-four hours away from Henry. The one time she had, he'd broken his leg so severely he'd needed a complicated surgery. How in the heavens was she supposed to send him to a summer camp where they got in kayaks and swam in the open sea for who knew how many days in a row?

"That's the answer to your question, Casey. I want to be with you and take the world by storm—all of us. Henry could do it with friends he makes in a place like this, and we could go on a trip together. Some place with a little more time to explore since he'll be taken care of. What do you think?"

"What do I think?" she asked. Her skin felt warm, then cool, and her voice didn't sound like her own. But that made sense since none of this sounded like her life. Leave her kid behind to travel and gallivant? No. Lawrence had wanted to "drop the tyke off" to her mother and jet to Europe to hike the Pyrenees and she'd balked then. Why would this be any different? "I think it sounds impossible."

Oh, no. He might be different from Lawrence in so many ways, but like she'd feared, this life wasn't enough for him. He'd always want more, wouldn't he?

Ian sighed. "I know it's hard to imagine living a life alongside your son, but you're allowed to do that, Casey. You're allowed to be happy, too." She knew that. And she was, most of the time. "I love you and want there to be more to this thing we're building."

Silence filled the cab, and she could hear her pulse in her ears.

"Love? You *love* me?" Her voice was shrill in the enclosed cab. She wanted to get out, to run, but where would she go?

"Yes, I love you. I love Henry, too." He frowned and she hated that she was doing this, that she was hurting him like this. "Don't you love me, too?"

"How can I? You want a life I can't give you—a life I gave up a long time ago. The woman you want isn't here anymore, can't you see that? You're trying to turn me back into her, but I'm only going to disappoint you when I can't follow through."

"You won't. And follow through on what? I'm not asking for anything other than for you to talk to me about this. I want to be with you and negotiate how we do that so we can care for each other the way we have been." His voice was strained but so were her nerves.

"For now," she said. "But Henry's life isn't up for negotiation. Can't you see that? Can't you see that you're going to get tired of giving up your life for him and me and leave us behind like…" She hesitated. "Like he did."

His jaw was set, twitching in what looked like anger. Good. Maybe that's what she needed; to make him mad enough to see she wasn't worth all this, that she was only saving him in the end.

"I'm not your late husband, Casey. Haven't I proven that so far?"

He had. But… "For what? A month? What happens when there's a big trip six months or a year from now and you want to go? I'll be a jerk if I need you here to help with Henry and I won't go back to that life where I feel guilty for keeping you from your dreams. I won't."

He tried to take her hand, but she refused it. Her skin itched and now it was too hot.

"I'm not asking you to, Casey. You changed the dream, can't you see that?"

She opened the door. Instantly, the laughter from the kids filled the air.

"No," she whispered. "I can't." She stalked off toward the side of the bay where there weren't any kids.

Part of her avoided glancing over at them because…what if? What if she watched them having fun and let it infect her enough that she let Henry come? And what if something happened to him? She'd never let herself be that selfish before and she sure wasn't going to start now.

"Where are you going?" he asked, following her.

"Can you just let me show you the camp? I think, even if you don't want to go away, you'll like it. We could even compromise and stay on island as well, in our own camp spot. This is a great way for Henry to feel like he's got agency in his own life—"

"Do not tell me what my son needs or doesn't need. Do you hear me? I've been his parent for five years and you've known him, what? Five *weeks*?" Ian's face reflected a deep sadness. She cringed at her own cruelty. But they couldn't continue. Not like this.

"I don't see what time has to do with this. I care about him, and you. I want to build a life with you both, can't you see that?"

The only thing she saw was how different their views were on what that life should look like.

"I'm going to have my mom pick me up, okay? I like you, Ian. A lot. And I think you're an amazing man. But—"

"Everything you're about to say makes that moot, doesn't it?"

Her chin hit her chest. "I'm sorry. I just think we're too different to make this work." She'd always sensed that, and today was the final proof she needed to protect her heart, but also Henry's and Ian's. He'd see that someday.

He cleared his throat and wouldn't meet her gaze. "I don't agree," he whispered, his voice thick with emotion. She couldn't let that influence her decision. She had to be strong enough to let him go. "But I respect your decision. Are you sure I can't at least give you a ride home?"

She shook her head. She was minutes from losing the battle of keeping her tears at bay. There was no way she wanted him to witness that.

"Thank you, Ian. And thank you for what you've done for Henry. I hope we can be adult about this so he can still come into the office and see me—and you."

"But to be clear, you don't want to see me anymore." It wasn't a question so much as a fact. She did want that, but didn't see a way to make it work. So she did what she promised him she'd never do—she lied.

"No, I don't."

"Okay," he said. "And you don't love me."

This lie was unforgiveable because it was the biggest one of all.

"No," she repeated. "I don't." Her heart screamed that it wasn't true, but her face betrayed nothing. She could love him all day long and still not want the risk that they might not work out. What if they kept this up and Henry grew more attached? It would only hurt worse down the road.

"Got it. Can I give you a ride home at least? We can talk about things?"

She shook her head. "I don't think so. My mom can come collect me. Please. I need to be alone, Ian."

He looked as if he might protest, but then he shoved his hands in his pockets and gave her one last teary look before getting in his truck and driving away. The moment he was out of sight, she broke down in tears. Somehow, her mom picked up on what she'd needed and where she was and got Erin to stay with Henry while she picked Casey up.

The wait could have been two hours or twenty minutes. Casey lost track of time as she zoned out looking over the water. Henry really would love it there. Maybe someday, when he was older, when she'd taught him more skills to keep himself safe…

Her mom arrived and wrapped her in a big hug before getting back in the driver's seat.

"What happened?" her mom asked.

"I don't want to talk about it," she whispered. The hurt was too fresh, too raw.

"Okay. I'm here when you do."

Casey's frown remained through the drive and lunch stop. Look at what that had done. She was ruining both their lives with her inability to be something more.

Someone she used to be.

The whole way home, she replayed Ian's words. He'd said "we" and brought Henry into the mix. He'd had a whole different view of what constituted safety for her son, and bristled when she disagreed with him.

That's not entirely true.

It sort of was. Let's say she'd agreed and they'd

gotten more serious. Would he truly want the life she was capable of living? It's not that she was saying he was like Lawrence—she was secure enough in her past to recognize that she'd settled for a man who liked pursuit more than appreciating the moment. Ian was good, and driven, and beautifully devoted to his community, herself included. But he was also a man who had grown used to living a life where he was only accountable to himself. What happened when this life, *her* life—of doctors' appointments, surgeries, caution—caught up to them? When she needed to cancel the fun to be responsible?

He'd go along with her view of things to keep her happy, but at his expense. That wasn't fair to any of them. Say they were out hiking, and Henry was at camp, or with her mom, even. What would happen to him if she had a fatal accident like Lawrence had? She was all Henry had left.

"Maybe that was the wrong question," her mom said eventually when they were almost home. "How *are you*?"

Oof. That hurt. Because she should be great, should be able to shout from the top of every canyon wall that she was happy, that she'd fallen in love.

That last realization was like a scalpel slicing through her heart. She knew the answer before he'd even asked the question. She loved Ian, and that's why she needed to set him free. Not just for him, but so she didn't always wonder if she'd made his life worse by tying him to a family that needed more attention than he could give.

"I'm fine," she said, her voice wavering with her own realization that…she wasn't. "I just can't do this anymore."

As she filled her mom in on the story, tears fell and her chest constricted, cutting off any air. Her mom just sat in silence when she was done, staring stoically out the windshield.

"I love you," was all she said to Casey, who choked out a sob. She was crumbling—not just from today and the loveliness she knew she couldn't keep, but from a lifetime of *almosts*.

She'd almost been happy so many times. And truly in her heart, she was content. She loved her son with every fiber of her being, loved practicing medicine nearly as much. She had a good relationship with her mom and a new set of friends. Life was lovely and dear to her.

It was also just not quite enough. She'd been great with what she had, until Ian came into the picture. He'd shown her what more was possible and what her days could look like, if only.

If only you have the courage to grab it and take a little risk. The rewards could be beautiful. But she couldn't afford to take that risk, not with all that was at stake.

When they arrived at Casey's house, Erin gave

her a sympathetic hug before she left. Henry was already asleep, so Casey slumped into the couch.

Her mom sat beside her and wrapped a loving arm around Casey's shoulder.

"Am I wrong or does it seem like we've been through a week's worth of days in the past twenty-four hours?" Casey asked. She laughed, but it sounded hollow, even to her. Her mom gave her a weak smile that she didn't deserve.

She'd joked to break the ice, but she wasn't lying, though. It had been a long day. A long series of days.

Maybe that's what she needed. Just…rest.

She leaned into her mom like she used to do when she was Henry's age. Just like before, her mom brushed back her hair and rubbed her forehead until the creases smoothed. When was the last time she'd let someone take care of her like this?

Ian just did last week. You were sick and he brought you soup and that latest romantic comedy with the actress from your childhood.

He was so good to her. Why couldn't she accept that love, though? Why couldn't she trust it?

Because it had never stayed. Not once.

"I'm just going to say this once, Case, because you're the smartest woman I've ever met, and I think on some level you already know it." Casey swallowed hard, not sure where this was going. Knowing her mom, they were about to have a "life is beautiful, take what you can get while you can get it" talk. Casey had done that her whole life until she was pregnant with Henry. Then it was time for her to put him first and be the mom he needed and deserved. Why couldn't everyone see that she was doing the best she could with what she had to work with?

"Okay," she whispered.

"You're doing it wrong." Casey blanched. Her forehead scrunched in protest but her mom shook her head, indicating she wasn't done yet. "Not wrong according to Henry or me, or even what society wants from you. But you're doing it wrong for *you*."

"I don't know what you mean. What's wrong with living to protect my son?"

Her mom smiled. "Nothing, Case. Not a darned thing. But there is something to be said for not remembering the woman that got pregnant with Henry in the first place. She was wild and beautiful and took the world by storm. She didn't let anything scare her, and now..." Her mom sighed and took her daughter's hand in hers, squeezing it. "I think the thing that drives you to make all your choices is fear. Fear about Henry, what will happen to him and what it will do to you if he gets hurt."

"Isn't that what a mom is supposed to do?" she whispered. But even as she said it, she knew it wasn't what her mother had meant. Still, the words stung. Maybe not because they weren't true, but because they were.

Ian wasn't Lawrence, and fear wasn't a way to make choices. Lawrence had made it easy for Casey to devote all her time to her son, not just because Henry needed it, but because her marriage wasn't what she'd needed regardless. Nor was it what Lawrence had wanted. He'd made that clear and…so had Ian. Ian did want her, and Henry. He'd done nothing but prove that over and over and she was letting her past dictate how she responded to that love, that care.

How fair was that to any of them? So she'd played a hand and lost. Why couldn't she sit back down at the table and let life deal her in again?

Because of Henry. Because no matter what, he needs more than other kids.

"You deserve to let yourself live, but even if you're silly enough not to do that, you owe it to Henry to let him live, too. To make his own choices and mistakes and to fall down and yes, get hurt. To be a boy who turns into a man one day."

Casey thought about that, her skin tingling with dread. That truth stung as much as the lies she'd told Ian. Which begged the question—was Casey wrong in thinking the way she did? It was her life, and something she'd learned when she'd buried Lawrence was that as an adult, she wasn't in trouble anymore for the choices she made for herself.

She could turn down invitations, accept that her life was in service of her son, and no one was going to be mad at her. Even Lawrence, when he'd been alive, hadn't been mad. No, he'd merely moved on and let her live the way she'd chosen to live.

But that meant the *almosts* she'd accumulated were her own fault. If she wanted to move past them and get what she really wanted in life, she had to be willing to leave her old life behind.

It was scary as all get-out, but so was staying paralyzed with fear as her mom had accused her of. Like both her mom and Ian had articulated, Henry deserved her bravery so he could forge his own.

That led to another realization. She could afford to make small risks because she had a partner in life who would support her and—this was the tough part to accept, but she did it with an open heart—not let her fall on her face. He'd be there to catch her if she let him.

She said good-night to her mom and went to work on a way to make things right with Ian. She could just eat crow and tell him she'd been rash and wrong. Or she could find a way to tell Ian—a man she trusted enough to take the risk to love—in a way he'd hear her.

She loved him and was willing to change to show him. Now, she just had to figure out what that looked like.

Ian finished opening up at the clinic and unlocked the front door. He'd volunteered to open shop all week, mainly to avoid being home. There, he was faced with the loneliness of his mistakes and the ramifications of them. Namely, the lack of Casey's long, blond hair draped across his chest in the morning while they cuddled, and the plate of left-overs in the fridge because he'd thawed enough salmon for both of them. Mostly though, he just missed the woman. Period.

Henry, too. And Scout, of course.

That's why, when the doors opened right after he'd turned around from unlocking them, and he heard Henry's voice, he froze before turning around. Sure enough, it was Henry, Scout and Casey, whom he hadn't seen in the two days since leaving her behind on Orcas Island. That had damn near killed him, driving home alone and knowing they were breaking up. All because he'd had a dumbass idea about what it meant to be a partner and start a family. What did he know about it?

"Ian!" Henry called, and used his crutch to maneuver himself over to Ian and into his arms. Ian was careful not to squeeze too hard, even though he was superexcited to see the boy.

"How are you, kid?" he asked. He hated that his voice cracked and he choked up. Would it always be this way around these two? He tried not to focus on Casey, standing at the entrance, but that would be like avoiding looking at a Grade A steak after a famine.

She looked beautiful, dressed in a T-shirt and hiking pants, her hair pulled back in a loose braid. She looked ready for adventure and his heart thumped against his chest. It only worsened when he met her gaze and she smiled at him. Why did his damned traitorous body have to register that as hope?

"I'm great. I'm going camping," Henry told him.

"Oh yeah?" Ian offered his hand as a high five even though the news surprised him—not in a bad way at all, though. This is all he'd wanted for the boy. Henry leaped up and lightly slapped it. "Where are you going?"

"Orca Island," Henry said.

"Orcas," his mom corrected him. He just nodded along. "And we're all going if you're interested."

He stared at her, so many questions at the tip of his tongue. They'd been so good at reading each other's minds when it came to that, but she didn't offer anything for him to go on.

"Who is 'we'?" he finally asked. She smiled.

"The three of us. Our little family, if that's still on the table for discussion."

The hope took flight and soared wildly out of control in his chest.

"Um, it is." He swallowed and took a step toward her. She met him with one of her own. "But I have to work today. When do you leave?"

"Now," Henry said, taking Scout by the leash. "After we both go to the bathroom, Mom said."

Erin came in. "Hey, Henry," she said, winking at Ian. "Can you show me Scout's new tricks?"

"Heck yeah!" He put his hand over his mouth and Ian hid a smile. "But yeah, 'cause he can shake now."

He and Erin headed for the back courtyard, leaving Casey and Ian alone.

"You don't work, unless you want to," she told him, taking another step forward. "I asked Greg to take your shift so we could spend some time together. I understand I have a lot of apologizing to do for how I treated you earlier this week, and so many times before that. But I'm hoping you'll allow me to do it on the trip instead, so we can make the morning ferry."

He forced his lips to go flat, his eyes not to betray his emotions.

"No," he told her. "You can't."

She shivered out a sigh and nodded. "I get it. I'm sorry, Ian. And I hope you have—"

She was in his arms as fast as he could get to her. "No," he said, kissing her. Shock registered in her rigid posture, but she loosened in seconds. "You can't ever apologize because there isn't anything to apologize for. You're an amazing mom and I jumped the gun, asking for something I had no business asking for. But we've got time and I need to tell you something. Something that has been on my mind since Orcas Island. The ferry doesn't leave for an hour. Can we talk?"

She nodded, and though her eyes were lined with worry, he continued.

"I want to thank you," he said. Confusion spread on her face. "You and Henry brought me back to surgery that I used to love. I'll never stop being grateful for you as a colleague and Henry as a patient."

She frowned. "Oh."

He laughed, then kissed her. "But," he added, "I'm more excited about this idea of a family you talked about. I made some choices about how I thought life made sense before I met you because of my sister. She never got to live her own life, so I think in a sense I was living mine for her. The risks, the adventures, the travel…it was so I could experience what she never would. All of it was just a bandage on a gaping wound, though."

"How so?" she asked. He took her hand and kissed the top of it. She smiled and it warmed his skin more than the sun coming in through the windows. It was a beautiful Pacific Northwest day.

"I thought living alone was the least risky, but I was wrong. Risk isn't bad—it's a barometer for what's worth your energy and what you're willing to give up to get what you want. And I want you and Henry."

"You do?"

He nodded and kissed her. "I know if my sister were here, she'd agree that's something she really would have wanted—a sister and a nephew. And on that note, I need you to hear me—I'll never, never leave you or Henry behind to take some stupid risky trip. I'm not—"

"I know you're not Lawrence. You're not selfish or uncaring. You've never shown us anything other than love and trust. I'm sorry I ever compared you to him. Or lied to you."

"How did you lie to me?"

"By telling you I didn't want you," she whispered. She leaned in and kissed him softly. "Or that I didn't love you."

He chuckled and pulled her into him. "I'm not going anywhere, Casey. Whether you choose me or don't, I'm in for this life with you and Henry—and I'll never stop putting you first. You're all the adventure I want, okay?"

"Okay," she said. A smile blossomed on her lips, and he couldn't keep from touching her as if his life depended on it. "Does that mean—"

"That I still love you, too? That nothing has changed in that department except me loving you even more? Yes to both. And that I want to come camping with you? Absolutely. Does it also mean that I want you every day for the rest of my life—all three of you? Hell yeah. If you'll have me, Casey, I'll make sure we spend every day of our lives building trust and loving."

"That's not good enough," she said. Now it was his turn to frown. What the…? "I want adventures with you, too, Ian. And Henry. What is life worth, like you said, without a little risk? So we won't say yes to you unless you promise to still get a little lost with us from time to time. Okay?"

"To quote Henry—heck yeah."

She laughed and wrapped her arms around his neck, kissing him deeply.

"Ew," Henry said, coming back into the room. "You guys touch each other's lips?" They shared a laugh and Ian knelt down in front of the little man.

"We do because we love each other. Do you know what that means?" he asked.

Henry nodded. "Love means you want to make the other person feel safe and happy."

Ian hugged him. "That's exactly right. I love your mom and you, which means I want to make sure you're both happy and safe for the rest of your lives. How does that sound?"

"Can we still go on the kayak?" Henry asked. The adults both nodded and held each other's hands. "And do I have to kiss you on the lips?"

Ian laughed heartily and shook his head. "No, sir, you do not. That's just for the adults."

"Then yeah, that sounds pretty cool, I think."

"I think so, too," Casey added.

Ian picked him up and the three of them shared a gentle group hug.

"I love you guys," he told them. And he always would. This was going to be a helluva new adventure for them all, and just like all the ones that came before, Ian felt nervous and calm at the same time.

That's how he knew that no matter what, this was going to be worth it. Love, as it turned out, was the one risk always worth taking.

EPILOGUE

"DAD," HENRY CALLED. "I need you!" His voice activated Ian, who jumped up from his seat at the backyard table where he'd been having a beer with Reese and Greg. He ran to the swing set, relieved to see Henry laughing and swinging with his Aunt Erin, his mom sitting beside him in her own swing, a baby cuddled in her arms. Ian's heart swelled each time he saw his family—all of them. He didn't think he'd ever tire of hearing the name "Dad" from the son he'd just legally adopted, either. He'd earned a spot on *Medicine Today*'s cover, won the prestigious Harper Medicine award for innovative work in the field, and still nothing brought him as much pride as being Casey's husband and Henry's father. Little Maddie's, too.

"One more push?" Ian asked.

"Two, please," Henry negotiated. His smile was positively mischievous, in the sweetest way possible.

"You got it, kid." He pushed Henry higher on the swing and though Casey watched them, she'd long ago lost the fear that used to line her eyes when

Henry played hard. They were careful, sure, but they'd all agreed it was best for Henry to live and play like the kid he was.

Since Henry had turned eight, he'd become both a curious and fun-loving boy as well as a mature young man who doted on his surprise baby sister—the gift they'd gotten the Christmas before when they'd mistaken Casey's missed period for perimenopausal symptoms.

Nine months later, the completion of their family unit had joined them, and Henry was thriving in his new role, too. Not just as a big brother, though there wasn't anything he wouldn't do for his baby sister to "keep her safe," and of course, spoil her with his toys and affection.

Ian met Casey's gaze and smiled.

"Can I get you anything, Mrs. Matthews?" Her smile was as wide as the day she'd taken his name two years earlier, their families and friends there to bear witness to the start of the greatest adventure Ian had ever taken on.

"I'm good, thanks, love. I think I might go put this little one to bed, though, since we're leaving so early tomorrow."

The four of them were about to head up to the San Juan Islands to do a camping trip, where Henry would stay four days longer with the OI camp he'd been to the past two summers. It was his hope to be a counselor like "Awesome Mike," who he'd met the previous year.

Ian and Casey couldn't wait to see what their son did with his beautiful life. And, thanks to the medical interventions he was brave enough to endure, Henry would have a long life if they had anything to say about it.

"If you want, I'll meet you back there," Ian said, throwing her a wink. "Leave the grilling to Reese." He was never sated with his desire for his wife, either. They had a chemistry that was undeniable and provided all the adrenaline-spiking he needed most days.

Erin choked on her wine. "You'll do no such thing, Matthews. My lovely husband is good at a lot of things but not quite the grill. Also, ew."

They all laughed as Erin got up to join her husband on the patio.

"I love you, Mrs. Matthews. Do you know that?"

She stood from her swing and handed him their daughter.

"I love you, too, Ian. More than yesterday and less than tomorrow."

Henry leaped from his swing, and landed softly in the sand they'd put under his playset.

"I love you both the most," he said. "Now who wants to race me to the sodas?"

His parents both put their hands up and ran with the boy, his sister tucked safely in Ian's arms, toward their future.

* * * * *

Look out for the next story in the
High Altitude Docs trilogy
Coming soon!
And if you enjoyed this story, check out these
other great reads from Kristine Lynn

City Doc to the Rescue
Doctor's Nine-Month Rival
Wedding Date with Dr. Petrides

All available now!